THE WHISPERING WOMAN

Paula Rivers, a beautiful, haughty young cinema cashier, is selling tickets when her sister Eileen delivers a portentous note to her: *'Be careful. People who play with fire get badly burned. Sometimes they die.'* Not long afterward, Paula is found murdered in her booth, shot from behind. Who was the haggard old woman dressed in black who had accosted Eileen and told her to give Paula the note? Called to investigate, Superintendent Budd is faced with one of the most curious mysteries of his career.

GERALD VERNER

THE WHISPERING WOMAN

Complete and Unabridged

LINFORD
Leicester

First published in Great Britain

First Linford Edition
published 2017

A catalogue record for this book is available
from the British Library.

ISBN 978–1–4448–3349–2

Published by
F. A. Thorpe (Publishing)
Anstey, Leicestershire

Set by Words & Graphics Ltd.
Anstey, Leicestershire
Printed and bound in Great Britain by
T. J. International Ltd., Padstow, Cornwall

This book is printed on acid-free paper

1

The Marcasite Box

Mrs. Rivers came wearily up the narrow staircase carrying a cup of tea on a tray. She was a small, dried-up, wizened woman with lines of care and trouble deeply graven in her face, and grey streaks in her lifeless, mouse-coloured hair. Reaching the square landing, she paused for a moment to recover her breath, and then softly opened the door of her daughter's bedroom and went in. The room was in semi-darkness.

A faint light percolated dimly through the thin curtains, grey and cold like the morning outside. Mrs. Rivers put down the tray on the top of a chest of drawers, and going over to the window, pulled back the curtains. The additional light which came flooding in lit up the room in all its incredible untidiness. Shoes and stockings lay strewn about the floor, intermingled with frilly underwear. A crumpled brown suit and a woolly coat had been thrown down carelessly in the armchair; and another, smaller chair was laden with hats and gaily coloured scarves. Most of the drawers were half-open, their contents partly overflowing, just as a last hasty rummage for some article or other had left them. On the floor by the side of the bed sprawled a pale green evening gown, lying as its wearer had stepped out of it on the previous night.

Mrs. Rivers looked at the litter and sighed. *She* would have to tidy up this room when her daughter had left it and gone to work; smooth and fold the rumpled clothes and restore them to their proper places in wardrobe and drawers. Paula was really very thoughtless, and she seemed to get worse instead of better. It would have been so easy for her to put her things away herself and save her mother so much extra work. Eileen, Paula's sister, was different. Her room was always neat and tidy, and she kept it clean herself, though she had less spare time than her younger sister. But then Eileen always had been different, even as a small child. Paula, because she was beautiful, had always expected everyone to run about and dance attendance on her, and nearly everyone did.

Mrs. Rivers sighed again, picked up the tray and went over to the bed. For a moment she stood looking down at the woman who lay there asleep, her red-gold hair streaming in shining waves over the pillow. Even the discontented, petulant mouth did not detract a great deal from her loveliness.

'Wake up,' said Mrs. Rivers. 'Wake up, Paula. You'll be late!'

Her daughter moved restlessly and murmured something, but her eyes remained closed.

'Wake up, Paula,' repeated Mrs. Rivers more loudly, bending down and gently shaking her by the shoulder. 'It's ten o'clock. You'll have to hurry.'

The pencilled brows contracted in a frown and the eyes, heavy with sleep, opened reluctantly. Paula blinked, yawned, and struggled up onto one elbow. 'Oh, I'm so tired,' she murmured huskily, pushing back the hair from her face.

'Drink your tea,' said Mrs. Rivers. 'It'll wake you up. You must have been very late last night, dear. I never heard you come in.'

'It was about two, I think.' Paula took the tea and drank gratefully. 'I've got a dreadful headache, Mother. Get me some aspirins, will you? There's a bottle on the dressing-table somewhere.'

Mrs. Rivers walked across to the littered dressing-table and began to search among the collection of face creams, powder boxes, bottles of lotion, nail varnish, and the hundred and one odds and ends that were jumbled together in hopeless confusion. 'Where did you go?' she asked.

'Up to town — dancing,' answered her daughter shortly. 'Can't you find them?'

'I don't know how you expect anyone to find *anything* among all this rubbish,' complained her mother. 'Why can't you be neat and tidy like Eileen?'

'Because I'm not made like Eileen, I suppose,' retorted Paula crossly. 'Eileen's content to hugger-mugger along in this ghastly house, wash her own stockings and clean her room, and generally moulder her life away. But I'm not. I want money — lots of money — and beautiful clothes, servants to wait on me, a car — everything that makes life worth living.'

'Well, I don't know how you expect to get it,' said Mrs. Rivers with a sniff. 'It's as much as we can do to make ends meet as it is, with your wages and Eileen's and what I make out of my sewing.'

'I may get it sooner than you think.'

'What do you mean?' Mrs. Rivers looked round quickly and anxiously.

'Never mind what I mean,' snapped her daughter. 'For heaven's sake, hurry up and find those aspirins — my head's splitting.'

'I wish you wouldn't say such silly things, Paula,' said her mother, resuming her search. 'You don't know how it worries me.'

'You needn't worry. I know how to take care of myself.'

'Your head's full of such big ideas,' said

Mrs. Rivers, shaking her own disapprovingly. 'And you've been worse since you've been working at that cinema. I suppose it's all those films.'

'Nonsense, Mother,' said Paula irritably. 'I've always been the same. I've never been content like you and Eileen. I know what I want, and I mean to get it.'

'Well, I'm sure I don't know how you're going to. Why don't you put all these stupid ideas out of your mind and marry Jimmy?'

'And live in a tiny, poky little flat on six pounds a week and bring up a family? Not for me, thank you.'

'Jimmy won't always earn as little as that. He's saving up to open a garage of his own. And anyhow, six pounds a week is not so little. There's lots of people who live on less. When I married your father, he was getting half that amount.'

'Yes, and look where it's brought you,' retorted Paula.

'I should have been all right if your father had lived.'

'But he didn't, and you had to bring up Eileen and me on practically nothing. I remember everything we went through; all the pinching and scraping. I remember when we were cold and hungry because we had no money to buy coal and food. And that's never going to happen to *me* again.'

'I'm sure it never would if you married Jimmy Redfern. He's a hard-working, steady lad, and — '

'Forget it, Mother,' said Paula impatiently. 'If you want Jimmy in the family so badly, get Eileen to marry him. She'd jump at the chance.'

'Paula!' exclaimed her mother, genuinely shocked. 'How can you say such things?'

'So she would. She's crazy about him. Look here, Mother, if you can't find those aspirins, don't bother anymore.'

'I've got them,' said Mrs. Rivers. She paused, and added in a different tone: 'Where *did* you get this, Paula? I've never seen it before.'

'What?' asked Paula indifferently.

'This pretty little box.' Her mother turned round and held it up. 'It's marcasite, isn't it?'

'Put it down!' cried her daughter shrilly and angrily. 'Put it down!' She sprang out of bed, ran over, and snatched the object of Mrs. Rivers's admiration from her hand.

'What on earth is the matter?' demanded her mother in resentful astonishment. 'I wasn't doing any harm.'

'I'm sorry,' muttered Paula a little shamefacedly. 'But you know how I hate anyone messing about with my things.' She pulled on a dressing-gown over her flimsy nightdress and slipped the little box into one of the pockets. 'Go and run my bath, will you, Mother? If I don't get a move on, I'm going to be terribly late.'

'What about your aspirins?'

'I'll see to them,' said Paula quickly. 'Go and run my bath, there's a dear.'

Mrs. Rivers obeyed, puzzled and a little angry. Why had Paula made such a fuss because she had picked up the little box? Where had she got it? And what had she meant by saying she might get all she wanted sooner than she expected?

Mingled with her curiosity and annoyance, Mrs. Rivers suddenly experienced a fresh sensation — a sudden unaccountable and altogether alarming sense of fear and foreboding.

2

Jimmy Redfern

Paula came quickly out of the little house in Eden Street and hurried along the wet pavement, her high heels click-clacking loudly. It was a dingy little street with a double row of drab-looking houses all exactly alike; and even on a fine day, with the sun flooding the narrow roadway, it was colourless and dreary.

Paula hated it. It represented for her everything that was sordid and ugly. She had played there as a child, more often than not cold and hungry, with other children equally cold and hungry, and had grown up with one deep-rooted desire and determination — to get as far away from Eden Street and its dismal and unpleasant counterparts as quickly as she was able. And now a chance had presented itself — a wonderful opportunity that had come miraculously out of the blue.

She hadn't paused to consider the right or the wrong of it. All she knew was that an almost unbelievable sum of money could be hers for the asking, and she had not been slow to ask. That there was an element of risk in what she was doing did not worry her very much. Her mind was too full of dreams and plans for the future to find time to listen to the faint warning voice which tried to make itself heard. By tomorrow she would be rich. That was all that mattered. All that her heart and soul had desired and craved for so long would be hers. It would be difficult to explain to her mother the source of this sudden wealth, but she hoped to be able to think of some convincing story. The truth she dare not divulge to anyone.

She was so completely absorbed in her thoughts as she turned the corner into the main thoroughfare and walked quickly toward the imposing entrance to the Mammoth Super Cinema, where she worked as chief cashier, that she failed to notice the man who was standing under the neon-crusted portico and who came eagerly to meet her as she approached.

'Paula!'

She came out of a land of mink coats and luxury flats, soft lights, music and glittering restaurants, with a start. 'Oh, it's you,' she said crossly. 'What do you want? Why aren't you at work?'

'I took an hour off,' answered Jimmy Redfern. 'I wanted to see you, Paula. What happened to you last night? I waited for over an hour.'

'I couldn't make it,' she said curtly. 'I can't talk to you now, Jimmy. I'm late already.'

'You never seem to be able to talk to me now,' he said bitterly, falling into step by her side. 'I don't know what's come over you lately, Paula.'

'I don't *have* to talk to you, do I?' she snapped ungraciously.

'You used to want to,' he said quietly.

'Maybe I did,' she retorted, 'but things change.'

'You mean you've changed?'

'If you'd rather have it that way — yes.'

His dark, lean, good-looking face twitched. 'Where did you go last night?'

he asked abruptly.

'That's my business. Look, Jimmy I must go. I'm nearly half an hour late as it is.'

They had reached the portico of the cinema and automatically came to a stop facing each other.

'You might at least have let me know you wouldn't come,' he said reproachfully.

'I meant to, but I forgot,' she said, staring past him at the shops on the other side of the street.

'Can I see you tonight?'

She shook her head quickly. She couldn't tell him, but that night was to see the triumphant culmination of all her plans — or so she fondly believed.

'Tomorrow night, then?'

Again she shook her head.

'Well, when *can* I see you?' he demanded urgently. 'Look, Paula, I've *got* to have a talk with you.'

'I don't know. What's the use, anyway? There's nothing to talk *about*, is there?' She saw the hurt expression in his eyes and, because she knew that she was being unfair and treating him badly, it roused all her irritation and annoyance. 'Why don't you stop pestering me?' she burst out angrily.

He looked at her — a long, searching look that epitomized all the cold misery within him. 'If that's how you feel about it,' he said huskily, as though all the moisture in his throat had suddenly dried up, 'there *isn't* anything to talk about.'

'I'm glad you realize it,' she retorted. 'Now I'm going. Goodbye.' She turned abruptly, pushed open one of the glass swing doors, and disappeared inside the vestibule of the cinema.

Jimmy Redfern stood for a moment staring blankly after her, his hands clenched tightly in the pockets of his raincoat, and then he swung on his heel and walked dejectedly away.

Paula ran up the broad flight of steps between the two pay-boxes that led to the circle foyer, her forehead creased in a frown. The unexpected meeting with Jimmy had come like a splash of cold water to waken her from her rose-tinted dreams of the future. So far as he was concerned, she wasn't behaving very well, and the knowledge made her feel uncomfortable. As a consequence, she was angry with herself — but angrier still with him, the innocent cause of her discomfiture. There had been a time when Jimmy Redfern had meant a good deal in her life; when she had been only too glad to let him take her about to dances and theatres and cosy little meals at the Greek restaurant up the street.

'Ullo, Miss. The guvnor's bin lookin' for you.' Mr. Foxlow, the foreman, came out of the circle entrance from the men's staffroom, already dressed in the magenta and silver uniform which the proprietors of the Mammoth Cinema provided for their employees. It was a little too big for his meagre figure, which rather detracted from its impressiveness.

'I'm late,' said Paula hurriedly and unnecessarily. 'I'll be down as soon as I've taken off my hat and coat.'

Foxlow looked after her with disapproval in every line of his sharp, thin face. Although he ruled over the usherettes and male attendants with despotic rigour, he had no jurisdiction over the cashiers and, as a result, bitterly resented what he called their 'h'airs an' graces.' As he slowly descended the circle stairs, his gimlet eyes on the lookout for any signs of skimping in the cleaning of the polished brasswork, the manager, Mr. Emanuel Benstead — a middle-aged, baldish man, running to fat — came out of his office which opened directly onto the vestibule.

'Have you seen anything of Miss Rivers, Foxlow?' he asked sharply.

'She's just come h'in, sir,' said Foxlow, contriving by the tone of his voice to express exactly what he thought of such dilatory behaviour.

'About time, too,' grunted Benstead. 'Where is she now?'

'H'up in the women's staffroom takin' off her 'at an' coat.'

'Hm!' Benstead pursed his rather thick lips. 'I'll have a word with her when she comes down. Who was responsible for cleaning the shillings this morning?'

Foxlow looked up at the big centre chandelier with considerable concentration. 'That'd be Mrs. Miller, sir,' he said with slow deliberation.

'Well, you tell Mrs. Miller to be more careful with the ashtrays. They haven't been properly emptied. Most of 'em have still got ash in them. Each one ought to be wiped clean, every morning.'

'I'll see to it, sir. Mrs. Miller skimps 'er work if you don't watch 'er.'

'Well, watch her!' said Benstead irritably. 'That's what you're paid for.'

'I'll do my best, sir. But h'it's impossible for a man ter be h'in 'alf a dozen places at the same time.'

'You'd better make it possible, or you won't be in any place at any time!' snapped the manager. 'Oh, good morning, Miss Rivers. Do you know you're nearly three-quarters of an hour late?'

'I'm so sorry, Mr. Benstead,' said Paula, hurrying down the steps breathlessly. 'But I wasn't very well this morning. I woke up with a dreadful headache.'

'Well, don't let it happen again,' said Mr. Benstead mildly. 'I suppose you can't help it if you don't feel well. Too much dancing and late nights. That's the trouble with all you young women.'

Foxlow sniffed expressively through his thin nose. He'd known she'd get away with it. Got away with murder, they did, them stuck-up cashiers.

Paula, guessing what was passing through his mind, smiled sweetly at him as she followed Mr. Benstead to the office.

3

The Message

It was the usual practice at most of the big cinemas for the chief cashier to combine her own job with such secretarial duties as might be necessary, and for the rest of the morning Paula was kept busy typing letters. At half-past twelve, half an hour before the cinema opened to the public, Mr. Benstead went up to the circle foyer to inspect the staff, which Mr. Foxlow had paraded in uniform for this purpose, and to issue such instructions as he desired. Meanwhile, Paula collected the return book, her five-pound float, and went into pay-box A to check the automatic ticket machine and take her starting numbers.

The pay-boxes at the Mammoth were on each side of the broad steps leading up to the circle, box A on the right as one entered from the street, and box B on the left. The upper half of each was built of ground glass, open at the top, and enclosing the cashier on two sides, the fronts containing an oblong opening through which the tickets were issued and change given. The sides nearest the two entrances to the stalls were of polished wood with a narrow door to admit the cashier, which could only be opened from the inside except with the key, which was kept by the manager. The back of each box was also of wood, and formed one side of a cupboard in which the ticket stocks were stored. Anyone going up or coming down the stairs to the circle could look down into the boxes — and, if they leaned over the brass handrail and were so disposed, just touch the head of the cashier.

Except on Saturday and Sunday, box B was seldom opened in the afternoon, all tickets being issued from box A; and it was Paula's custom to open up and remain on duty until two o'clock, when Grace Singer, the second cashier, arrived and took over while Paula had an hour's break and went out to lunch.

She came back at three and stayed in the box until four-thirty, at which time Grace again relieved her until five-thirty. At six o'clock, the beginning of the busy period, box B was opened to handle the circle seats only, with Grace in charge of it, and the two women then remained at their posts until half an hour after the start of the last screening of the big picture. Then both boxes were closed, and Paula cashed up, checked her returns, and took cash and return book in to Mr. Benstead for his final check and signature. That, so far as Paula was concerned, was the end of the day's work.

Usually at opening time there were not many people to deal with, but today was early closing, and there was quite a queue for the cheaper seats. For half an hour Paula was kept fairly busy, and then the stream of people slackened to a trickle.

A few minutes after the doors opened, she saw her sister Eileen come into the vestibule, and wait for an opportunity to come over and speak to her. She was a tall, slim woman with honey-coloured hair, two years older than Paula; and although she lacked her sister's vivid beauty, there was something about her that was very attractive. *If only she would take more trouble with herself, she'd be lovely,* thought Paula. *But she looks washed-out, and her hairstyle's terrible. Why doesn't she try to be smarter?*

When there was a lull at the pay-box, Eileen came quickly over. 'I say, Paula,' she greeted her sister excitedly, 'such a funny thing happened just now. I'd just left the shop when a queer old woman came up to me, thrust an envelope into my hand, and asked me to give it to you.'

'An old woman?' said Paula, frowning. 'What was she like?'

'Like a witch out of a fairytale,' said Eileen. 'A gaunt old creature dressed in shabby black. And she had such a queer voice — a sort of husky whisper as if she had a very bad cold, or laryngitis, or something of the sort. Who is she?'

Paula shook her head. 'I haven't the faintest idea. I don't know anyone like that. Did you say she gave you an envelope?'

'Yes. Here it is.' Eileen produced it

from her bag and pushed it into the pay-box. 'Look — it's addressed to you, 'Miss Paula Rivers'.'

'Two one-and-sixes, miss, please.' A little group of people had collected suddenly while they had been talking, and Eileen stood aside while Paula dealt with them.

'Now,' said Paula when they had all gone in, 'let's see what this is all about.'

It had crossed her mind that it might be a message from Jimmy Redfern begging her to see him, but the writing on the envelope was not his. She ripped it open, drew out a sheet of paper, and read the single line that was scrawled across it.

'Oh!' she gasped faintly. 'Oh.'

The watchful and curious Eileen saw her face go white under her make-up and the colour on her cheeks stand out in two vivid, unnatural patches. 'What is it, Paula?' she asked anxiously. 'What's the matter?'

Her sister recovered herself with an effort. 'Nothing. It's . . . it's nothing. Only a — a bill that I thought I'd paid.' She crumpled the letter into a ball and thrust it into the pocket of her jacket. 'Are you going in?' she said, changing the subject abruptly and striving to speak normally.

'Well, now I'm here I suppose I might as well,' said Eileen. 'I say, you look awfully sick, Paula.'

'I'm all right,' said Paula, but her voice was a little shaky. 'Go on up to the circle, Eileen. Helen's on the door. She'll let you through.'

'Come and collect me when you have your tea break, and we'll have some together,' said Eileen as she went up the steps.

'O.K.,' said Paula. She looked up as Eileen reached the circle foyer, and her sister waved down to her.

It was meant as a little friendly gesture. Neither of them had the remotest idea that it was destined to be a gesture of farewell.

4

The Woman Who Whispered

Mr. Emanuel Benstead sat back in his office chair, rubbed his tired eyes gently, and then lit a cigarette. He had got through a lot of work since he had come down from the café after lunch, and his eyes ached a little. He had worked out the time-sheets for six weeks ahead and completed the copy for the local newspaper advertisements for the same period. That was as far as he could go, for the film bookings extended no further. However, it was a good afternoon's work, and he felt relieved that it was done and off his mind. A glance at his watch told him that it was nearly half-past four, and at half-past four either Grace Singer or Paula Rivers usually brought him his tea.

There was a tap at the door and Harry Stanton, the resident organist, came in. 'Is there an organ interlude the week after next, Mr. Benstead?' he asked.

'No, Harry,' answered the manager, looking at the time-sheets he had just finished making out. 'You're only playing at the opening, for the trailers. Can't get in an organ interlude for three weeks. There isn't time; the programmes are all too long. We'll have to open at twelve-thirty instead of one o'clock to get 'em in as it is.'

'That suits me,' said Stanton with a grin. 'I'm working up a new slide show, and it'll give me time to get it perfect.'

Grace Singer came in with a cup of tea. She was short, with a mass of rather coarse-looking black hair, and glasses.

'Thank you, Grace,' said Benstead as she set the cup down on his desk. 'You just going to relieve Miss Rivers?'

'Yes, sir.'

'I think I'll pop up to the cafe and get some tea myself,' remarked Harry Stanton, and he took his departure.

'What's it like outside?' asked Benstead, sipping his tea. 'Are we busy yet?'

Grace shook her head. 'There was nobody at the box office when I came by,

Mr. Benstead. They don't seem to like the film this week.'

'I can't say that I blame 'em,' grunted the manager. 'I think it's a lot of tripe.'

'Clark Gable's lovely, though. Would you like another cup of tea, Mr. Benstead?'

'Yes, please.' The manager held out the empty cup and she took it and went out. She hadn't been gone more than a few seconds when George Kenway, the chief operator, came in.

'There's a bit of a flutter in the sound-head of number two projector, guv,' he said. 'It's not very bad now, but it may get worse.'

'All right,' said Benstead. 'I'll phone up head office and get them to send the engineer down. What is it, d'you think?'

'Wants a new spring in the gate,' replied Kenway briefly.

Mr. Benstead picked up the telephone, dialled a number, and spoke rapidly into the receiver. 'Thompson's coming at ten o'clock tomorrow morning,' he announced when he had finished. 'How's that new lad getting on, Chief?'

'Stephens, guv?' said Kenway. 'I think 'e'll be all right. 'E's willin' and a good worker. I'll be getting back to the box, an' let Conway go for 'is tea.'

'H'excuse me, sir.' The nasal voice of Mr. Foxlow, alarmed and agitated, broke into the end of his sentence.

'What is it?' asked Benstead curtly.

'H'it's Miss Rivers, sir,' replied the foreman. 'Somethin's 'appened to 'er. She's bin took ill.'

'I'll come at once!' Benstead sprang out of his chair and hurried into the vestibule with Kenway and Foxlow at his heels. A little group of people stood in front of box A, watching an attendant who was peering in through the oblong opening. Grace Singer, with a cup of tea in her hand, alternately whimpering and offering suggestions, was hovering about just behind.

'What's the matter? What's happened?' demanded Benstead peremptorily, pushing his way to the pay-box.

'She's fainted, poor kid,' said a stout woman in a fur coat sympathetically.

'Looks more like a fit to me,' remarked

a lean, lugubrious man, shaking his head dolefully.

'Can't we go in?' demanded a thin, hard-faced woman irritably. 'We shall miss the beginning of the big picture.'

'Take this lady and her friend in, Foxlow,' snapped Benstead. 'We'll bring your tickets to you in a few minutes, madam.' He pushed the attendant away and took his place.

Paula was sitting slumped forward on her stool, her red head sunk on her breast, her arms resting on the metal top of the automatic ticket machine.

'Miss Rivers. Miss Rivers!' Benstead reached inside the pay-box and patted her on the arm. But she made no response, either to voice or movement. Not a little scared, but mindful that his first duty was to his public, the cinema manager swung round.

'Open box B, Grace,' he said; and to the attendant: 'Jarvis, tell everybody that the other pay-box will be open immediately, and that all tickets will be issued from there.'

'Whatever's the matter with her, sir?'

whispered Grace, white-faced and curious.

'I don't know. Something serious, I'm afraid,' answered the worried Benstead. 'Hurry up, woman, and open that other box. Take your numbers on a separate sheet of paper. I'll give you the book presently.' He pulled his keys from his pocket, unlocked the door of box A, and thrust the bunch into the hand of Grace. 'Go along and get that pay-box open,' he ordered.

She complied reluctantly, and Benstead squeezed himself into box A. There wasn't much room, and in order to get in at all he had to sidle behind the motionless woman balanced on the stool. And in doing so, he saw something that made him catch his breath and drained the blood from his fat face. The back of Paula Rivers's dark grey frock was wet and glistening in the brilliant strip lighting that surrounded the top of the pay-box.

He saw too, with growing horror, that in the centre of the patch of wetness there was a small round hole in the cloth.

Gingerly he touched the place, and when he looked at his finger he found that it was red and slightly sticky. Blood!

'Wot's the matter with 'er, sir?' inquired the voice of Mr. Foxlow from the door.

'I — I don't know,' replied Benstead shakily, 'but it looks as if she's been shot.'

'Shot!' The foreman's voice rose almost an octave.

'Be quiet!' snapped Benstead urgently. 'Do you want to let everybody know? This has got to be handled carefully. Get hold of one of the men and send him for a doctor. Then come back here and guard this box while I telephone for the police.'

Foxlow, looking incredulous and alarmed, hurried away, and the harassed cinema manager switched out the light in the pay-box. With the place in darkness, few people would be able to see that there was anything wrong, and the longer this was kept from the public the better.

Benstead licked his dry lips and rubbed his suddenly clammy palms together. This was terrible. If Paula Rivers had been shot, it was murder. Somebody must have shot her from the circle steps or the foyer. But surely the report of the pistol would have been heard? And there were always at least two male attendants in the vestibule.

'Jarvis 'as gone for the doctor, sir,' said the foreman, returning.

'All right,' said Benstead, coming out of the pay-box and shutting the door. 'You stay here until I come back.'

'What's happened, guv?' asked Kenway.

'I don't know yet.' *Better not to say too much until the police arrive*, thought Benstead. 'Miss Rivers is — is ill. I've sent for a doctor.'

He hurried into the office and got through to the police station, explaining rapidly what had happened. The desk sergeant promised to send an inspector along at once. A little relieved now that the proper authorities had been notified, Benstead went back to the vestibule.

Grace Singer had opened box B and was dealing with a small stream of people who were trickling in from the street. To all outward appearances, things were going normally, which was something to be thankful for.

'Who was on duty in the vestibule this afternoon?' asked the manager, joining Foxlow. Kenway had gone, presumably back to the operating room.

'Slater an' 'Iggins, until they went ter their tea at three-thirty,' answered the foreman. 'Then Jarvis an' King took their places.'

'When did you notice there was anything . . . wrong with Miss Rivers?'

'Just afore I come an' told you. It were a patron what first drew me attention.'

'How long had you been in the vestibule then?'

'About twenty minutes. I'd just come back from me tea. Miss Rivers was h'all right then, sir. I saw 'er issuin' tickets to a couple o' people.'

'You didn't hear anything like — like the sound of a — a shot? Or any kind of noise?'

'Good lord, no, sir. H'everythin' were very quiet. It were a bit slack just round about then, sir.'

Benstead rubbed his fleshy chin. It was

incredible! Paula Rivers had been shot with three people standing a few yards away, and none of them had heard or seen anything!

'There was *one* thing, sir, now I come to think of it,' went on the foreman after a pause. 'I didn't take no account of h'it at the time, but . . . '

'Well, go on, man! What was it?' snapped Benstead impatiently.

'It were a queer little old woman. She come inter the vestibule just arter I got back an' 'ung about the place like as she might be waitin' for somebody.'

'Probably she was,' broke in the manager.

The foreman shook his head. 'No she weren't, sir,' he said. ''Cause, seein' 'er 'overing about uncertain-like, I asked as if there was h'anythin' I could do to 'elp 'er, an' she said: 'No, I'm just curious, that's all.' Jarvis called me over fer some string fer the tickets — the piece what he was threadin' 'em on 'ad broke — an' when I come back, she'd gone.'

'Hm! Would you know her again?' asked Benstead.

'Yes, sir. Though I h'ain't never seen 'er before. She were small an' wrinkled, an' spoke funny.'

'How d'you mean, 'funny'?' said the manager sharply.

'H'in a queer kind of a whisper, sir,' said Mr. Foxlow.

5

Mr. Budd Is Interested

Superintendent Robert Budd, that fat and lethargic man, was paying one of his rare visits to his area that day, and happened to be in the police station talking to Longfoot, the divisional inspector in charge, when the call came through from the Mammoth Cinema. The unusual circumstances of the crime and its background aroused his interest, and he elected to accompany the inspector on the investigation.

With some difficulty he squeezed his bulky form into the seat beside the driver of the police car, leaving the back to be occupied by Inspector Longfoot; Sergeant Ball, the police photographer; and the fingerprint man. The result was a fairly tight fit, but luckily the Mammoth Cinema was not very far away, and the short journey was accomplished without a great deal of discomfort. The divisional inspector had rung up the police surgeon before leaving the station, and the doctor's car arrived in front of the cinema almost coincident with their own.

There was little to suggest that anything unusual had happened when they entered the vestibule. A short queue of people was lined up in front of one of the pay-boxes, from which a woman was busily issuing tickets, and beside which stood a uniformed attendant.

The other pay-box was in darkness, and grouped before it were half a dozen people, obviously members of the cinema staff. From this group a short, stout man with a partially bald head detached himself and came hurriedly forward to meet them.

'My name is Benstead. I'm the manager here,' he said. 'I rang up the police. This is a terrible affair. I'm doing my best to keep it quiet from the public.'

'You seem to've done pretty well, sir,' remarked Mr. Budd, looking sleepily round. 'You say one o' the cashiers 'as been shot?'

Benstead nodded jerkily. 'Yes, in the pay-box. At least, I think she was shot. I sent at once for a doctor, but he hasn't come yet.' He strove hard to speak calmly, but Mr. Budd could see that he was very worried and agitated.

'It doesn't matter, sir,' he said soothingly. 'The divisional surgeon's 'ere. 'E'll be able to tell us.'

'I hope you'll try and keep this — this dreadful affair as quiet as you can,' said Benstead anxiously. 'I mean from the audience. I've been on to my head office, and the area supervisor is on his way here.'

'Don't you worry, sir,' said Mr. Budd cheerfully. 'We'll look after everythin'.' He turned to the divisional surgeon. 'You'd better get busy,' he said.

The doctor, a middle-aged man with glasses and a short greyish moustache, went over to the pay-box, and Benstead unlocked the door and switched on the light.

'If you all stand round the front,' he said, 'the people going in won't be able to see much.'

That was, apparently, his principal anxiety, and Mr. Budd thought it was quite understandable. Doctor Riley made a quick but thorough examination.

'The woman is quite dead,' he announced when he had finished, 'and she has undoubtedly been shot. The bullet appears to have entered her back, just below the left shoulder-blade, and is still in the body. I should say that it is probably lodged in the heart — I can tell you more about that after the autopsy. From the angle of penetration it would seem that the shot was fired from above, downwards. From somewhere up there, in my opinion.' He jerked his head towards the circle vestibule.

'Thank you, doctor,' said Inspector Longfoot. 'Now, sir, I shall be glad if you will give me an account of what happened, so far as you know it.'

'Certainly,' said Mr. Benstead. 'Perhaps you would like to come to my office?'

'I think that would be best, sir,' agreed the inspector. 'Hodges, you can get on with photographing the body. And take a picture of the whole vestibule, including the two pay-boxes an' the upper vestibule,' he added. 'You might get one *from* the upper vestibule, too, looking down.'

The photographer nodded and began to unpack his apparatus.

'You two fellows,' said Longfoot to the two uniformed constables who had just arrived, 'keep a guard on this pay-box, and don't let anyone get near it. Now, sir . . .'

'Keep an eye on the front, Foxlow,' said Benstead to the foreman, and he led the way to his small office.

The account he gave them was, in spite of his agitation, admirable for its clear and concise nature. Sergeant Ball took it all down meticulously in a large notebook, and when the manager had finished, stood stolidly licking the point of his pencil and waiting for his services to be required again.

'Interestin' and peculiar,' commented Mr. Budd, staring sleepily at a large green safe in one corner of the office. 'So there was no sound of a shot, eh?'

'Nobody heard one,' said Benstead, shaking his head. 'Which is rather queer when you come to think of it, considering that there were three people quite close.'

'Have you got a noisy programme this week, sir?' asked the inspector.

'In parts. But you wouldn't be able to hear much of it out in the vestibule.'

'If the killer used a powerful air-pistol,' murmured Mr. Budd thoughtfully, transferring his sleepy gaze from the safe to a tall stationery cupboard, 'nobody would've 'eard anythin'. An air-pistol would've been quite powerful enough at close range.'

'There's something in that, sir,' agreed Longfoot.

'There's a lot in it,' said the stout man. 'An' if the murderer's still in the cinema 'e, or she, 'as got the weapon with 'em.'

'Just a minute,' interrupted the inspector, and hurried out of the office. He was back again in a few seconds. 'I've taken care of that, sir,' he said. 'Everybody leavin' the cinema'll be searched.'

'Oh, I say . . . ' protested Mr. Benstead with a troubled frown.

'I'm very sorry, sir,' said Inspector Longfoot firmly, 'but it's got to be done.

It'll be carried out as tactfully as possible.'

'An' if you don't find anythin', you'd better search the buildin' as soon as it's empty,' said Mr. Budd.

'You must remember,' put in the manager, 'that there are a number of exits. A lot of people use them instead of coming out through the front.'

'Thank you, sir, I'll attend to that.' The inspector picked up the telephone and got through to the police station. After a short conversation, he put down the receiver. 'There'll be a man on each exit in a few minutes,' he said. 'Of course we may be too late — the murderer may have gone — but it's worth trying.'

''Ow long 'ad this gal, Paula Rivers, been in your employ, sir?' asked Mr. Budd.

'Nearly three years,' answered the manager.

'What sort of a gal was she?'

'She was very good at her job. A bit too fond of late nights — dancing and that sort of thing — but most women are these days.'

'Was she engaged?' asked the inspector.

'No,' replied Mr. Benstead. 'There was a young fellow she was pretty friendly with — a chap called Redfern — who used to call for her and take her home, or out somewhere.'

'Used to?' murmured Mr. Budd.

'Well, I haven't seen much of him lately. Not for nearly a month or more.'

'Hm,' grunted the big man. 'Did she go about with a lot o' men friends?'

'Not that I know of. This chap Redfern is the only one I've seen.'

'Send for your foreman, what's-'is-name — '

'Foxlow,' said the manager, getting up. 'Do you mind if I go and tell him? One of us ought to be on the front.'

'That's all right, sir,' said Mr. Budd; and as the manager hurried away: 'Queer business, eh, Longfoot?'

'Very, sir,' agreed the inspector. 'Of course, it may prove to be quite simple. Just a case of jealousy, or pique, on the part of this man Redfern.'

'Maybe,' said Mr. Budd, 'an' maybe not.'

There was a tap on the door and Mr.

Foxlow came in. 'You wanted me?' he said.

'Your name's Edward Foxlow and you're the foreman here?' said Inspector Longfoot, and Foxlow admitted that that was so. 'Tell us all you know about this business,' said the inspector, and Sergeant Ball prepared to get busy again.

Foxlow did so, his story tallying exactly with Benstead's. When he mentioned the queer old woman who had been hanging about the vestibule, Mr. Budd, who appeared to have fallen asleep, suddenly opened his eyes to their widest extent, a disconcerting habit of his when he was interested.

'She said 'I'm just curious,' did she?' he murmured. 'You're sure that's what she said?'

'Yus, that's what she said. Her voice was funny-like. Sort of a whisper, as though she'd got a bad cold,' said Foxlow.

'What 'appened to 'er?' asked Mr. Budd.

The foreman shook his head. 'I dunno. I didn't see the goin' of 'er.'

'For all you know, she might've gone

into the cinema?'

'She might,' said Foxlow doubtfully. 'But I'm pretty certain she didn't, as if she 'ad I'd've seen 'er.'

To Inspector Longfoot's surprise, Mr. Budd's interest in the old woman seemed inexhaustible. He extracted from Mr. Foxlow a minute and detailed description of her, and only when he had obtained this did he seem satisfied.

When they had finished with the foreman, Jarvis was sent for. He, too, had seen the queer old woman, but he was more emphatic than Mr. Foxlow that she had not gone into the cinema. He didn't know what exactly had happened to her, but he was quite sure she had not gone inside.

'You seem very interested in this old dame, sir,' said Inspector Longfoot when Jarvis had gone to send in King. 'D'you think she's important?'

'In the early stages of a case like this,' answered Mr. Budd sleepily, 'yer can't tell what's important an' what ain't. But when you strike somethin' that's out o' the ordinary, it's just as well ter find out all yer can about it. This old crone came because she was curious, an' soon after, a woman is shot dead. There may be no connection, but it makes *me* curious too.'

When they had questioned the other attendant, King, and the rather scared Grace Singer, whose duties in box B Mr. Benstead temporarily took over, they were in a position to fix, roughly, the time during which the crime must have been committed. Paula Rivers had been seen alive and issuing tickets at four-forty, and had been discovered dead at four-fifty. Whoever had fired the shot that killed her had, therefore, done so during that intervening period of ten minutes. This narrowing down of the time to so small a margin was going to be of considerable help in the investigation. Granting that the shot had been fired from the circle foyer — and this seemed fairly certain — it meant that only those people who could have been there between four-forty and four-fifty were suspect.

They left the office and went back to the vestibule. The queue in front of box B had increased to considerable dimensions, and Benstead and Foxlow were coping with it manfully. A large notice-board bearing a poster advertising the following week's programme had been brought from its usual place in the vestibule and propped up against the front of box A, so that nothing was visible of the dead woman inside.

'I hope you didn't mind?' said Benstead in a hoarse whisper, coming over to them. 'I was afraid somebody might see.'

'A very good idea, sir,' said Mr. Budd. 'Let's go an' take a look at the body, Longfoot.'

'You won't want me anymore, will you, sir?' asked the police photographer of the inspector. 'I've got the pictures you wanted.'

'O.K., Hodges,' said the inspector. 'You needn't stay either, Black,' he added to the fingerprint man. 'There's nothing for you yet.'

He joined Mr. Budd, and Benstead unlocked the door of the pay-box. There wasn't enough room for the big man to get inside, but he was able to see all that he wanted by leaning forward.

'Hm, there's nothing here,' he murmured. 'No reason why she shouldn't be moved, is there?'

No,' said Longfoot. 'Sergeant, cut back to the office and ring for the ambulance.'

Sergeant Ball nodded; and as he turned to obey, a woman came quickly down the circle steps and hurried towards them.

'Oh,' she gasped, 'is it true? About Paula?'

'Who are you, miss?' demanded Mr. Budd.

'I'm her sister . . . Paula's sister,' said Eileen, turning a white, anxious face from one to the other. 'It isn't true, is it? Helen says that Paula's dead. It *can't* be true . . . ?'

'Who's Helen?' asked Mr. Budd.

'Helen's the woman on the circle entrance,' said Benstead quickly.

'Was she there at four-forty?' queried the stout superintendent sharply.

'Yes,' answered the manager. 'She should've been there from two-thirty until five. She has a break at five of half an hour for tea.' He glanced at his watch.

'She must've just got back.'

'I want to see 'er,' said Mr. Budd.

'What *has* happened to Paula?' broke in Eileen. Mr. Benstead . . . ?'

'I'm afraid what the gal told you was right, miss,' said Mr. Budd gently. 'Your sister's been killed.'

Eileen uttered a startled sound that was half-cry, half-gasp. 'Killed?' she echoed incredulously. 'How? Was it an accident?'

'No, miss, it wasn't an accident,' replied Mr. Budd gravely. 'Your sister was shot.'

'Oh!' She stared at him, fear and astonishment in her wide eyes. 'You don't . . . you don't mean . . . she was murdered?'

'I'm afraid that's what I *do* mean, miss,' said Mr. Budd.

He expected some kind of an emotional outburst, but nothing of the kind happened. The shock of his words seemed to have the opposite effect. For a moment she continued to stare at him in silence and then she said in a voice that was quite calm and steady: 'Who did it?'

'We don't know, miss,' said Mr. Budd. 'That's what we're tryin' ter find out. Maybe you can 'elp us?'

'Me?' She moistened her lips quickly with the tip of her tongue, and the fear in her eyes deepened.

'Do you know of anyone who might 'ave a grudge against your sister?' he inquired, watching her under his heavy lids. 'Big enough to want to kill 'er?'

'No,' said Eileen. 'There was nobody. How could there be? Oh . . . '

He saw her face change. Some sudden recollection had come to her. 'You've thought of somethin', miss,' he said. It was a statement, not a question.

'The letter,' she said, frowning. 'The letter . . . perhaps *that* had something to do with it.'

'What letter is this?' asked Mr. Budd sharply.

'A queer old woman gave it to me just as I left work and asked me to give it to Paula,' answered Eileen.

'An old woman, miss?' said Mr. Budd, and he shot a quick look at the divisional inspector. 'What was she like?'

'Shabby and dressed in black, with a face like a witch,' replied Eileen. 'A dreadful old creature. She spoke in a funny, husky sort of whisper.'

'It's the same woman, sir,' interrupted Longfoot excitedly. 'It looks as though you were right.'

'Hm, it does, don't it?' murmured Mr. Budd. 'This woman stopped you, miss, when you was leavin' work, an' gave you a letter to give to yer sister?'

'Yes.' Eileen looked from one to the other in a puzzled manner. 'Why do you say it was the same woman? Do you know her?'

'No, miss,' said Mr. Budd, 'but maybe we will pretty soon. What time was it when this woman gave you the letter?'

'About twenty minutes past one. I came straight here and gave it to Paula. It seemed to upset her very much, as though it contained something that gave her a bad shock. That's why I thought it might have something to do with . . . with . . . ' She stopped, stammering for words.

'What did she do with the letter after

she'd read it?' asked the big man.

'She crumpled it up and put it in her pocket.'

'See if you can find it,' grunted Mr. Budd to the inspector. ''Ave you ever seen this woman before?'

Eileen shook her head.

'Hm, interestin' an' peculiar. Do you think yer sister knew 'er?'

'I'm sure she didn't. She looked very surprised when I told her who had given me the note.'

'Here you are, sir.' The divisional inspector came back with a crumpled envelope in his hand. 'It was in the right-hand pocket of her jacket.'

Mr. Budd thrust his hand into his breast pocket and pulled out an old pair of cotton gloves, which he put on. Then he took the envelope, frowned at the superscription on it, and gingerly withdrew the contents.

'Ah!' he said, when he had read the message on the single sheet of paper. 'Now we're gettin' 'ot, as the kids say. Take a look at that, but don't touch it. There may be prints.' He held it out so that Longfoot could read it.

'Be careful. People who play with fire get badly burned. Sometimes they die.'

'So Miss Paula Rivers was playin' with fire, was she?' murmured Mr. Budd. 'An' she *did* get badly burnt. That letter's a piece o' first-class prophecy. H'm, now I wonder just what kind o' fire she was playin' with?'

6

The Woman Who Called

Eileen Rivers's face had gone white and anxious, and there was a strained expression in her large eyes. It was a pity, thought Inspector Longfoot, that she was colourless. With a touch of make-up, and her hair done differently, she would have been a very pretty woman.

Mr. Budd put the note carefully back in the envelope and stowed it away in his pocket. "Ave you any idea what this letter meant, miss?' he asked.

Eileen shook her head. 'No,' she said, but Mr. Budd was not convinced by the denial. If she didn't know, then she had, during the few seconds it had taken her to read the warning, formed a shrewd idea, and it had shocked her. Her whole manner betrayed her mental agitation.

'What's happened? What's happened to Paula?' The voice broke in upon them sharply and unexpectedly. Eileen expelled her breath in a sudden gasp, and the colour flooded her cheeks for a moment and then receded, leaving them whiter than before.

'Jimmy,' she said. 'Jimmy . . . '

'What's the matter?' he demanded harshly. 'What's happened to Paula?'

'Is your name Redfern, sir?' asked Mr. Budd, remembering what Mr. Benstead had told them.

'Yes,' said Jimmy Redfern curtly. 'Will *somebody* tell me what's happened?'

''Ow did you know *anythin'* had happened?' said Mr. Budd. His question was addressed to Redfern, but he was watching Eileen. She was staring at the newcomer, and her eyes were dark with anxiety.

'Helen told me,' he answered impatiently. 'I was in the cinema, and she came and told me some rubbish about Paula having been shot.'

'Oh, Jimmy,' whispered Eileen.

'You don't mean it's *true*?' he said, turning on her quickly. 'My God, it can't be.'

'I'm afraid it is,' said Mr. Budd. 'You was a great friend of Miss Rivers's, wasn't you?'

'Yes, yes. We were practically engaged,' said Redfern impatiently. 'How did it happen? Who did it — '

'Shhh.' Mr. Benstead came hurriedly over to them. 'Keep your voice down, *please*. You're attracting the attention of the people going in.'

'Damn the people!' said Redfern rudely. 'I want to know.'

'There's no reason why yer shouldn't know quietly,' said Mr. Budd. 'We don't want ter make a song an' dance about this — not more'n we can 'elp.' Briefly he explained what had happened, and Redfern received the news in stunned silence, his lean white face eloquent of his grief.

'Paula,' he muttered huskily. 'Paula . . . It doesn't seem possible.'

'It's . . . it's dreadful, isn't it, Jimmy?' said Eileen, and he nodded dumbly.

'What time did you come into the pictures?' asked Mr. Budd.

'About a quarter past four,' Redfern answered mechanically, in a voice that sounded dry and throaty.

'Miss Rivers was in the pay-box,' said Mr. Budd. 'Did yer speak to her?'

Redfern shook his head.

'Why not? Surely you 'ad to get yer ticket?'

'I didn't buy a ticket,' replied Redfern. 'I had permission from Mr. Benstead to go in when I liked.'

'An' you went straight up the stairs ter the circle? You didn't even say good afternoon to Miss Rivers?'

'No.'

'A bit funny, ain't it?' suggested the stout superintendent. 'You was practically engaged to this gal, you say, an' yer come into the place an' pass 'er without even sayin' good afternoon?'

Jimmy Redfern flushed and looked embarrassed. 'I . . . we had a bit of a row this morning,' he muttered.

'I see,' remarked Mr. Budd, and he privately decided to go into the cause of this quarrel later. 'So when you last saw Miss Rivers, she was alive?'

'Yes. She was issuing tickets to some people.'

'Did she see you?'

'I don't know. I don't think so. If she did, she didn't take any notice.' He was obviously nervous and uneasy. Eileen, Mr. Budd noticed, was watching him anxiously. There was no doubt, he thought, how *she* felt towards this young man who hardly seemed aware of her existence. She was in love with him. An interesting situation, considering that he had been practically engaged to her sister . . .

'After you went inter the cinema,' he said, 'did you come out again — I mean, before yer come out just now?'

'Yes,' answered Redfern. 'I went to the gentlemen's lavatory in the circle foyer.'

'When?' asked Mr. Budd sharply.

'I don't know exactly . . . Round about a quarter to five, I think.'

'This gal — what's-'er-name — Helen? Was she at the circle entrance when yer did that?'

'She was inside talking to Doris, one of the usherettes.'

'So she didn't actually see you go to the lavatory?'

'She saw me leave the circle and she

saw me come back. What's the idea of all these questions?'

'Just a matter o' routine, Mr. Redfern,' said Mr. Budd blandly. He stepped forward suddenly and ran his hands with practised dexterity over the astonished young man. 'Nuthin',' he murmured to the divisional inspector. 'Would you mind openin' your handbag, miss?'

Eileen did so, showing her surprise at the request, and he peered inside.

'All right, thank you, miss,' he said.

'Look here, what's all this about?' asked Redfern angrily.

'We're doin' that to everybody leavin' the cinema. It's our belief that Miss Paula Rivers was shot with an air-pistol, or a pistol fitted with a silencer, an' we want ter find it.'

'But . . . good God! You don't think that either of us . . . ' said Redfern in consternation.

'I don't think anythin' yet,' interrupted Mr. Budd truthfully. 'I'm just collectin' all the facts I can at present. Do you know anyone answerin' to this description?' He described the shabby old woman in black with the whispering voice, but Redfern denied any knowledge of her.

'All right,' said Mr. Budd with a prodigious yawn. 'Where do you live, miss?'

Eileen told him.

'We'll go round there now,' he said. 'You'd better come along too, Mr. Redfern. You look after things 'ere, Sergeant. I don't want any o' the staff o' this place ter go until I get back.'

As they left the cinema, the ambulance arrived. Although it was only a short distance to Eden Street, Mr. Budd insisted on going by car. During the journey, he extracted from Eileen as full an account as he could of the Rivers household. Redfern had relapsed into a worried, rather sullen silence, and stared out of the window.

Mrs. Rivers came to the door of the little house in answer to their knock, and looked in surprise at the group on the step. 'Eileen. Jimmy . . . ?' She shot an inquiring glance at Mr. Budd and Longfoot.

'Mother,' said Eileen quickly. 'Oh Mother, it's Paula.'

'Paula?' The tired, lined face of the little woman grew suddenly anxious and apprehensive. 'What has she done?'

'It's dreadful, Mother . . . ' began Eileen.

'Has she been . . . been . . . Is there any trouble at the cinema?' broke in Mrs. Rivers. 'If she's taken any — anything that didn't belong to her . . . money . . . '

'Why should you think that your daughter 'ad taken money?' asked Mr. Budd.

'I — I — she said . . . ' Mrs. Rivers stammered incoherently in her troubled confusion.

'I think it 'ud be better if we came in, ma'am,' said Mr. Budd gently.

'Yes, yes . . . come in,' she agreed hurriedly, and stood aside while they crowded into the narrow hall. It struck Mr. Budd that Mrs. Rivers had spent the greater part of her life standing aside.

'Come in here.' She opened the door of a small, stuffy room that smelled of furniture polish and old carpets. 'What is it? Please tell me what's happened.'

'Paula's dead,' said Eileen, almost in a whisper.

'Paula — dead?' Mrs. Rivers stared at her, her thin lips slightly apart. 'Dead . . .' The corners of her mouth began to twitch.

Eileen put an arm round her thin shoulders. 'Don't, Mother,' she said. 'Please don't cry.'

'How did it happen?' said Mrs. Rivers huskily. 'Was it an accident?'

'No, ma'am, I'm afraid it wasn't,' said Mr. Budd. 'Your daughter was shot.'

Mrs. Rivers uttered a queer little sound like a choked cry. 'Shot?' she whispered in horrified surprise. 'Oh, no, *no*!'

'It's true, Mother,' said Eileen. 'Now, don't . . . don't . . . please don't, dear.'

The little woman, her face working, sank onto an uncomfortable-looking settee and began to cry piteously.

'Don't,' said Eileen softly, cuddling the grey-streaked head to her breast. 'Please don't, darling.'

'I — I can't help it,' sobbed Mrs. Rivers. 'I knew no good would ever come from all her high-flown ideas.' She broke into a paroxysm of weeping, and they stood silently waiting for the first flood of her grief to exhaust itself. There was nothing they could do to alleviate it. After a few minutes, the sobbing grew less and presently stopped. Mrs. Rivers took the handkerchief that Eileen gave her, then dabbed at her eyes and blew her nose.

'I — I'm sorry,' she apologized tearfully. 'I couldn't help it.'

'Of course you couldn't, ma'am,' said Mr. Budd sympathetically. 'It must've been a nasty shock for you. I'm sorry that we 'ave ter bother you at such a time, but I'm afraid it can't be 'elped. Now, do you think you feel able ter answer a few questions?'

Mrs. Rivers nodded dumbly. The tears were still running down her thin, lined face, but she was calm and more in control of herself. Her hand clutched Eileen's and she clung to it convulsively, as though by the very closeness of the contact she could draw strength and comfort.

With infinite tact and consideration, Mr. Budd began his questioning; and slowly from the stammered replies, which gradually became more and more coherent as he proceeded, he built up a picture of the Rivers' history. He also gathered a pretty shrewd insight into the character of the dead woman. Spoiled from childhood, she had grown up into a vain, selfish woman with one fixed determination — to acquire, at any cost, the money that was essential to gratify her craving for expensive clothes and the surroundings that went with them.

'I pleaded with her over and over again to put such foolish ideas out of her head, but she wouldn't listen,' said Mrs. Rivers pathetically. 'I wanted her to marry Jimmy and settle down and forget all that nonsense about West End flats and cars and servants to wait on her. If she'd only listened to me, this would never have happened.'

'Why do you say that, ma'am?' asked Mr. Budd quickly.

'Because I'm sure she was up to something she shouldn't have been,' declared Mrs. Rivers. 'All those late nights, not coming home till two or three in the morning — she was out until two last night — and then saying that she expected to get hold of a lot of money soon . . . '

'When did she say that?'

'This morning. I've been thinking and worrying about it all day. She was excited, like she used to be when she was a little girl before her birthday party. Flying into such a temper, too, because I asked her where she got the little box from. Oh!' She suddenly recollected something. 'If she was . . . killed at five o'clock, what happened to the little box?'

'What little box, ma'am?' inquired Mr. Budd softly.

'It was a pretty little box made of marcasite. I found it on her dressing-table this morning when I was looking for the aspirins. I'd never seen it before, and I asked her where she got it, but she snatched it out of my hand like a fury.'

'Where is this box?' asked Mr. Budd as she paused.

'The woman took it away with her,' said Mrs. Rivers. 'The woman Paula sent.'

'What was she like, this woman?' said

Mr. Budd with sudden interest.

'She was a queer old thing. Very shabby, and dressed in black, like a witch. I could scarcely hear what she said; she spoke so strangely — in a husky sort of whisper.'

7

The Air-pistol

There was no doubt that the woman who had called for the marcasite box was the same who had given the note to Eileen Rivers, and whom Mr. Foxlow had seen hanging about the vestibule of the cinema. She formed a kind of leitmotif throughout the whole business, and Mr. Budd decided that it was important for the police to get hold of her as quickly as possible. He made a mental note to have an all-stations call sent out to find and detain her.

After answering a few more questions, Mrs. Rivers's forced composure broke down and she relapsed into another fit of sobbing. Mr. Budd obtained permission to search Paula's room and went up alone, leaving the divisional inspector to keep an unobtrusive eye on Jimmy Redfern.

The dead woman's room was neat and tidy, a tribute to her mother's industry of the morning, and he made a thorough and methodical search. From what he had gathered from Mrs. Rivers, there seemed a distinct possibility that Paula, in her desperate desire for money, had become involved in something that had led to her death. Her remark of the morning, which suggested that she was expecting to acquire the money she craved in the immediate future, bore out this hypothesis, and it received further confirmation from the note the mysterious old woman had given to Eileen to deliver to her sister. Paula Rivers had got herself mixed up with something unsavoury and illegal, or both, and had paid for her folly with her life. She had 'played with fire', and the resultant burn had been fatal.

Mr. Budd hoped to find among her effects something that would give him a clue to the nature of this 'something' in which she had become entangled, but his hopes were not realized. There was nothing at all that even remotely suggested what it could be. After a diligent search, all he found to reward him for his efforts were two crumpled menu cards bearing the coloured picture of a flamboyant parrot and headed 'The Talking Parrot Club'.

The big man knew the place by its reputation, which was not particularly good. It was situated in a street off Piccadilly and conformed to the usual type. There was a band, a microscopic dance floor, and a bar. Colonel Hautboy, the proprietor, was a retired army man, and his record was not the best. He had done nothing to bring him into the law courts, but he had on several occasions sailed perilously close to the wind, and was marked by the police as a man worth watching. There were many such men in London, and sooner or later they made a false move and were swept into the net which Scotland Yard put out for such catches.

The membership of The Talking Parrot was a mixed one, for there was only one standard necessary to become eligible, and that was money. Everything at The Talking Parrot was expensive. The food was excellent — it was said that Colonel Hautboy paid his chef a salary that ran into four figures — and the wines were the best obtainable. Outwardly, at any rate, the place was conducted with the most meticulous observance of the law, though what went on behind this respectable façade was another matter. Colonel Hautboy lived in a flat above the club premises, and there were rumours that from here he controlled a number of profitable — and less legal — sidelines, but nobody had ever been able to substantiate them.

And this was the place to which the dead woman had been, not once but apparently several times. Not the kind of place one would expect to be frequented by a cinema cashier. Mr. Budd wondered who the man was who had introduced her. Obviously a member of the club, and just as obviously someone with plenty of money. The Talking Parrot was impregnable to any other kind.

The superintendent went downstairs to the stuffy little sitting-room to find Inspector Longfoot and Jimmy Redfern the only occupants. Eileen had persuaded her mother to lie down and was making her a cup of tea.

'We'll be gettin' back to the cinema,' said Mr. Budd wearily. 'I think you'd better come with us, Mr. Redfern.'

The young man looked at him as though he was going to refuse, but apparently thought better of it and followed them out into the hall. 'Goodbye, Eileen,' he called.

'Come back later, won't you, Jimmy?' she said, coming out of the kitchen.

He hesitated.

'Do,' she urged. 'You haven't had anything to eat. I'll make you some supper, and we can talk.' Her eyes pleaded silently, and rather grudgingly he assented.

'All right,' he said. 'I'll come.'

She smiled, and Mr. Budd caught a fleeting glimpse of a loveliness that was far greater than Paula's rather exotic and flamboyant beauty. Young Redfern must be a blind fool not to see it too, he thought.

Sergeant Ball had news for them when

they reached the cinema. A man had been detained for further questioning in the manager's office. 'You'll never guess who it is, sir,' he said to Inspector Longfoot. 'An old friend of ours.'

'I'll buy it,' said the divisional inspector. 'Who is it?'

'Ted Figgis,' said Ball with a grin.

'Figgis, eh?' murmured Mr. Budd. 'Now that's very interestin'.'

Ted Figgis occupied a unique place in that substratum of the community that was popularly referred to as the underworld. The professional crook, as a rule, stuck to one particular form of crime: the confidence man would not dream of committing a burglary; the forger would have nothing to do with anything outside his special graft; the smash-and-grab specialist would confine himself solely to his own rough-and-ready method of making a nefarious living. The rigid rule of the 'cobbler sticking to his last' was adhered to with punctilious care by the majority of criminals. But Ted Figgis was the exception. He had tried everything that could be expected to yield easy money, from 'whizzing' to blackmail; had appeared at irregular intervals at most of the London police courts to answer charges that were both varied and surprising, and had spent fifteen years out of his forty-five in prison.

He was a tall, rather distinguished-looking man with thin fair hair, a large thin nose, and eyes that were a peculiar pale shade of blue. When they entered Mr. Benstead's office, he surveyed them with an expression of haughty annoyance.

'This is an outrage,' he said. 'An outrage! I demand an explanation.'

'You'll get it, Figgis,' said Mr. Budd, regarding the immaculate grey suit that Mr. Figgis was wearing with admiration. 'You look almost like a gentleman. You must be doin' well. What's the latest graft?'

'I don't know what you mean,' replied Mr. Figgis with dignity. 'Why have I been detained? It's outrageous.'

'You've said that before,' interrupted Mr. Budd. 'Don't repeat yourself, Figgis.'

'The reason we detained him, sir, was this note,' said Sergeant Ball. 'We found it in his pocket.'

'It's a scandal!' declared Mr. Figgis. 'You had no right to search me.'

'Everybody's bein' searched,' retorted Mr. Budd curtly. He took the paper the sergeant held out to him. On it he read in typewritten characters:

> *'Mammoth Cinema, Regent Road, at four forty-five. Don't fail. Rivers will be no longer a danger.'*

In place of a signature had been neatly drawn the outline of a parrot.

'Very interestin' indeed,' remarked Mr. Budd. 'Maybe you can explain this, Figgis?'

'Why should I?' demanded Figgis truculently. 'Isn't this a free country?'

'Up to a point,' replied the big man. 'But not when it comes ter killin' people it ain't.'

'I don't know what you're talking about. I haven't killed anyone.'

'There was a gal murdered 'ere this afternoon,' said Mr. Budd. 'She was shot, an' the time she was shot was roughly four forty-five. 'Er name was Paula

74

Rivers. That's what I call somethin' like a coincidence.' He tapped the note in his hand significantly. Ted Figgis's sallow face went a lighter yellow, and into his pale eyes sprang an expression of alarm.

'I know nothing about it,' he said quickly. 'I didn't know anything of the sort had happened.'

'The person who sent you this message did,' said Mr. Budd. 'I should say 'e knew *all* about it. Who was it?'

'To tell you the honest truth,' declared Figgis with great candour, 'I don't know. A man I'd never seen before came up to me in the street, put that note in my hand, and walked away. He must've mistaken me for somebody else.'

'I'll bet he did,' said Mr. Budd sceptically. 'Why did yer come 'ere if the message wasn't fer you?'

'Pure curiosity. But I don't suppose you'll believe me.'

'I don't s'pose I shall,' declared Mr. Budd with conviction. 'In fact, I don't mind tellin' yer I don't. Is Colonel Hautboy a pal o' yours?'

'Colonel Hautboy?' Figgis frowned.

'No, I don't think I know the name.'

'Ever 'eard of The Talkin' Parrot?'

'The Talking Parrot?' repeated Figgis. 'I seem to have heard the name somewhere.'

'I'll bet you 'ave, an' I'll bet you've 'eard of Colonel Hautboy as well. Now suppose you come clean an' tell us the truth?'

'I assure you,' said Figgis earnestly, 'that I've told you all I know.'

'I see. That's your story, an' you're stickin' to it, eh? That some unknown man gave you this note in the street in mistake for somebody else an' that's all you know about it?'

'That's the truth,' said Figgis doggedly.

'Take 'im along ter the cooler,' ordered Mr. Budd. 'Figgis, you're detained on suspicion of bein' concerned in the murder of Paula Rivers, an' anythin' you say may be used in evidence. There, that's all straightforward an' above-board. Now take 'im away.'

Figgis protested and threatened, but all to no purpose. In the charge of a stolid constable he was led away, still arguing violently.

'Maybe a few hours in a cell'll make 'im talk,' said Mr. Budd callously.

'There's not much doubt he knows something,' said the divisional inspector, 'though I'm not sure he had anything to do with the woman's death.'

'No more am I,' agreed Mr. Budd. 'But I'm pretty sure he knows why she died. This gal Paula Rivers was a flighty type, an' she wanted money so badly that she was willin' ter do most anythin' ter get it. It's my belief that she found out about some graft that was goin' on, an' tried ter put the black on the people what was runnin' it. Instead of payin' up, they bumped 'er off. An' this feller Figgis is mixed up in it.'

'And Colonel Hautboy and The Talking Parrot?' said Longfoot.

Mr. Budd nodded slowly. 'Yes, I think so. That seems ter be the place this gal went to when she didn't come 'ome until two or three in the mornin'.'

'Excuse me, sir.' A youthful-looking policeman thrust his head in at the office door. 'I've just found this, sir.' He came in, his face flushed with triumph, and showed them a peculiarly shaped pistol with a long, thin barrel, which he held gingerly in a handkerchief.

'An air-pistol!' exclaimed the divisional inspector. 'Where did you find this, Harriman?'

'In the gentlemen's lavatory,' replied Constable Harriman, 'in the circle foyer. It was on the top of the cistern.'

8

The Compact

Eileen Rivers turned down the gas under the boiling kettle until it was a microscopic blue flame. The cloth was laid on the kitchen table, and a dish of sausages and bacon was keeping hot in the oven. She hoped that Jimmy Redfern would not be long, or the supper would be spoiled. She ran upstairs and peeped into her mother's bedroom. Mrs. Rivers, exhausted with weeping, was asleep.

Eileen returned to the kitchen and sat down in a chair by the table. She felt very tired and her head ached dully. She wished that Jimmy would come, because she was very worried about him. It was surprising, she thought, that *he* should be her chief concern. It was terrible about Paula, but she had very little feeling in the matter. It might almost have been a stranger who had been murdered, and not her own sister, for all the grief she could summon up. It was true that she and Paula had never been very close companions. They had been too entirely different in temperament for that; but she ought, she thought, to feel more upset over her death than she did.

It worried her a little, this lack of sentiment. There seemed something indecent about it. But she couldn't conjure up an emotion that wasn't there. The trouble was that it *ought* to be there, and all that *was* there was a vague feeling of relief. She was shocked at having to admit it even to herself, and wondered whether it had anything to do with Jimmy Redfern. Paula had treated him so badly, and yet he'd had eyes for nobody but her. Perhaps now . . . She felt herself go hot at the thoughts that surged into her mind. It was wicked to feel almost glad that an obstacle had been removed, and yet she couldn't help it.

A knock came on the front door, and she got up quickly and hurried along the passage to answer it. It was Jimmy.

'I wouldn't have come if I hadn't

promised,' he said wearily.

'I'm glad you did,' she said. 'I've got some supper all ready for you, keeping hot in the oven, and the kettle's boiling to make some tea. Take off your coat and sit down.'

He did so, dropping dejectedly into a chair. His eyes were tired and his face looked thinner and drawn. He had the appearance of a man completely exhausted.

'I hope your supper isn't dried up,' she said, busying herself at the oven. 'I expected you earlier.'

'It's lucky I'm here at all. I thought they were going to arrest me when they found the pistol.'

'Where did they find it?' she asked, setting the dish of sausages and bacon before him.

'Behind the cistern in the gentlemen's lavatory,' he said. 'I don't think I can eat anything, Eileen, really.'

'Try,' she urged. 'It'll do you good. Why should they want to arrest you because of that?'

He told her. 'They put dozens more

questions to me,' he said. 'Made me tell them how, when, and why I quarrelled with Paula.'

'But Jimmy,' she broke in, 'they can't be so ridiculous as to think *you* did it.'

'Can't they?' he said grimly. 'That's just what they *do* think. The only reason I'm not in clink now is because they're not sure. But I'll bet you there's a detective outside this house, watching to see that I don't make a bolt for it.'

'Well if that's the case, we've just got to do something about it,' said Eileen, pouring boiling water into the teapot.

'What can *we* do?' he demanded.

'Find out who really did kill Paula,' she answered calmly, and he stared at her.

'That's all very well,' he said after a pause, 'but how can we do that?'

'I don't know. But we can try, can't we? That old woman who gave me the note to give Paula — she must know a good bit about it. Couldn't we try and find her?'

He looked a little dubious. 'The police'll be looking for her,' he said. 'They'll find her before we do.'

'Well if they do, so much the better,'

said Eileen, pouring out two cups of tea. 'But in case they don't, there's no harm in us trying as well. *Do* eat something, Jimmy. It'll do you good.'

'What about you?' he asked.

She felt that anything solid would choke her, but she answered: 'I will, if you will.'

'All right,' he said listlessly, and drew up his chair to the table.

She helped him and herself from the dish of sausages and bacon and sat down.

'You know,' he said, sipping the hot tea, 'I can't realize it yet — that Paula's dead. It doesn't seem possible, does it? She was always so full of life.'

'I know, Jimmy,' she said sympathetically. 'You were . . . very fond of her, weren't you?'

He nodded, his eyes on his plate. 'I'd have done anything for her, anything in the world. It was queer, the effect she had on me — a kind of infatuated fascination. I couldn't get her out of my mind, and yet there were times when I hated her.'

'Jimmy!'

'Oh yes, I did,' he went on, stabbing at

a portion of sausage with his fork. 'She used to get me so mad I could've killed her.'

'You'd better not let anybody hear you say that,' she said apprehensively.

'No, you're right.' He ate a little food mechanically and drank some more tea. 'What *was* Paula playing at?' he said. 'Where did she expect to get all this money from?'

Eileen shook her head. 'I don't know. She never confided in me, not about anything. For all I knew about her, she might have been a stranger.'

'It was only recently, wasn't it, that she got this idea?'

'She always wanted money and clothes and expensive things,' said Eileen, 'ever since she was old enough to want anything. She always hated living here in the way we do. But it was only since she started going out at night that she began to drop hints that she might get what she wanted soon. It worried Mother dreadfully.'

'Who did she go with?'

Again Eileen shook her head. 'She

never said. I know where she went, but not who took her.'

'The Talking Parrot. A posh West End nightclub.'

'How did you know that?' she asked in surprise.

'From that fat fellow — Budd, or whatever his name is. He asked me if I'd ever been there with her.'

'Well, that's where she used to go, and that's where all the trouble started.'

'I'd like to know just what it was she'd got herself mixed up in,' he muttered. 'It must've been something pretty serious for the people concerned with it to . . . to have . . . ' He left the sentence unfinished.

'Let's try and find out, Jimmy. Couldn't we go to this club one night and — '

'They wouldn't let us in,' he objected, but a gleam of interest had come into his dark eyes. 'You have to be a member to get into those places.'

Eileen's face clouded with disappointment.

'I'll tell you what though,' he said

suddenly. 'There's a customer at the garage, a fellow called Nicholls, who runs a Lagonda and has got heaps and heaps of money — he's probably a member. He belongs to most places of that sort. I've heard him talking about it. Perhaps he'd take us in. He's a cheery, good-natured sort of chap.'

'Why don't you ask him?' Eileen said, her eyes sparkling.

'I will. It'll cost a good bit, but I've got nearly three hundred saved up, and I may as well spend it now.'

She knew what that money had been intended for, and understood the bitterness in his voice. 'I've saved some money, too — ' she began.

'You keep it,' he interrupted. 'I'll foot the bill. I don't mind spending the lot, if we can get to the bottom of this business and find out who the swine were who killed poor little Paula.'

Eileen felt a thrill of elation. She had succeeded in rousing Jimmy out of his apathy, and the fact that they were in this together added to her pleasure. She had a momentary twinge of conscience that she should feel so happy in the circumstances, but she resolutely smothered it. Paula would understand.

'You said you'd eat something if I did,' Jimmy reminded her, 'and you haven't touched a thing.'

'All right, I will. Would you like some more tea?'

Between them they finished the contents of the dish, although it had got cold, and they both felt better. Jimmy produced cigarettes, and they sat smoking and talking and making plans until it was quite late.

'You're a good sort, Eileen,' he said when at last she escorted him to the door. 'You've cheered me up a lot tonight.'

'I'm glad, Jimmy. I've cheered myself up, too.'

'We'll find out the truth between us. We won't give up until we do.'

'That's a bargain,' she said, holding out her hand.

'It's a bargain,' he agreed, taking it firmly. 'So long.'

'So long, Jimmy,' she said, and stood at

the door watching him as he strode off down the street.

A man who had been standing on the other side of the road came out of the shadows and followed him. So he'd been right, Eileen thought with a slight dampening of her spirits. The police *were* keeping him under observation. She came slowly in and softly shut the front door.

9

The Talking Parrot

It was very late that night before Mr. Budd had finished at the Mammoth Cinema and left with Divisional Inspector Longfoot, Sergeant Ball and the police constables who had been assisting them. The entire staff had been subjected to a most intensive questioning designed to extract every atom of information that was available concerning Paula Rivers and the movements of every individual during the important period from four-thirty to five o'clock. But the result was not very enlightening. The majority of the staff had, apparently, disliked the dead woman. She had 'given herself airs', and generally behaved as if she considered herself superior to the rest of them.

At least six of the persons so patiently questioned had had an opportunity to fire the fatal shot: Helen Mills, the woman who had been on duty at the circle entrance; Kenway, the chief operator; Harry Stanton, the organist; Mr. Foxlow, the foreman; and Jarvis and King, the two attendants. They had all been in the immediate vicinity of the circle foyer at one period or another during the ten minutes in which the murder must have been committed. But there was no evidence against any of them.

Of all the people concerned, the most likely suspect was Jimmy Redfern. He had been in love with Paula and she had turned him down. There had been a quarrel, and it was quite plausible that he had killed her in a fit of jealous rage. He had left the circle to go to the gentlemen's lavatory within a few minutes of the actual moment when the shot must have been fired, and the air-pistol from which it had come had been found in that lavatory on the top of the cistern. The divisional inspector was almost convinced that they need not look any further than Redfern, but Mr. Budd was sceptical. If Redfern was guilty, it left too many loose ends unaccounted for, and he was of the opinion that there was something bigger behind this murder of a cinema cashier than the act of a jealous lover.

At the same time, he agreed with Longfoot that the young man should be kept under close observation. He had rung up Colonel Blair, the assistant commissioner at Scotland Yard, to report on the crime, and since he had been present at the initial investigation, had received official instructions to take charge of the case. He quickly had taken the opportunity of putting out an all-stations call to hold and detain the shabby old woman in black with the whispering voice. Her evidence, if she could be found, he was convinced would be of the utmost importance; for she obviously not only knew what Paula Rivers had contemplated, but was aware that she was in danger.

The area supervisor of the circuit that owned the Mammoth Cinema — a big, stout man for whom Mr. Emanuel Benstead seemed to possess a kind of reverential awe — was not in the least interested in discovering who had killed the chief cashier. His one and only desire was, apparently, to get the police out of the cinema as quickly as possible and restore it to its normal conditions. He had growled and grumbled at everybody, reduced the unfortunate Benstead to a condition of dithering nerves, and finally took his departure, having contrived to make himself a general nuisance to everybody and contributed not one iota of help. Mr. Benstead came back from escorting him off the premises, wiping his perspiring forehead.

'All he kept saying was, why hadn't I dressed?' he said plaintively. 'Good Lord, have I had time to change with all this?'

They left him, a weary and worried little man trying to check his returns, and Mr. Budd reached his small villa at Streatham at a quarter to one and went to bed.

He was up early on the following morning and at Scotland Yard before nine. When Sergeant Leek put in an appearance, he found the big man sitting at his desk in his cheerless little office staring ruminatively at his blotting-pad.

'Ullo,' he greeted. 'You're early, ain't yer?'

'Any time before noon seems early ter you,' grunted Mr. Budd. 'Don't stand there with the door open; come in an' shut it. There's a hell of a draught.'

Leek obeyed, shambling over to a chair and perching himself on it.

'Ever 'eard of The Talkin' Parrot?' asked Mr. Budd, glowering at the window.

'I knew an old lady once what 'ad one,' said Leek brightly. 'It used ter say 'Come an' kiss me, Charlie' as natural as — '

'I don't want to 'ear your immoral reminiscences,' snarled Mr. Budd, cutting him short. 'The Talkin' Parrot is a nightclub off Piccadilly.'

'I know the place yer mean,' said the sergeant. 'It's run by an American feller — Captain Oh-boy.'

'That's right. Only 'e ain't an American, he ain't a captain, an' his name's Hautboy.'

'Oh-boy *is* American — ' began Leek argumentatively.

'It ain't 'Oh-boy'!' snapped his superior. 'It Hautboy — spelt H-A-U-T-B-O-Y.'

'Oh, *Hawtboy*,' corrected Leek with great complacence.

'It's pronounced 'Hoboy',' explained Mr. Budd wearily.

'Silly way ter pronounce it, I think. What about 'im?'

'We're goin' ter pay him a visit. Ternight.'

Leek's face fell. 'I was taking me evenin' off ternight.'

'Well, yer can just put it on again. I'm goin' to The Talkin' Parrot an' you're comin' with me.'

'What for?' demanded the sergeant, and the stout superintendent explained.

'Rummy sort of business, ain't it?' commented Leek, when he had finished a brief account of the case. 'That's the worst of these 'ere modern young gels, yer know. They're always gettin' themselves tangled up with trouble. Now, when I was a boy . . . '

'I know the story of Adam an' Eve,' cut in Mr. Budd. He took a brown paper parcel from his desk. 'Now make yerself useful and take that along to the F.P. Department, an' get 'em to test it fer prints. When you've done that, 'ave it checked up by the firearms experts, an' then set inquiries goin' to find out where it was bought an' who bought it.'

Leek took the parcel and looked at it curiously. 'What's this?' he asked.

'It's the air-pistol that Paula Rivers was killed with,' said Mr. Budd patiently. 'What did yer think it was, a pea-shooter?'

''Ow was I ter know?' began Leek indignantly. 'I — '

'Oh, get along an' do as you're told!' snarled the exasperated Mr. Budd, getting up and reaching for his hat. 'I'm goin' out.'

He went no further than a certain little tea-shop in Whitehall of which he was a regular habitue. Here, over a cup of coffee, it was his custom to work out his ideas and ponder over the aspects of a case until he had evolved a rough working hypothesis. Today he had come for information. The man he had arranged over the telephone to meet was sitting at a table in one corner, and the stout superintendent waddled over and joined him.

'Ullo, Barry,' he greeted. 'What's all the latest scandal?'

Barry Race grinned. He was a middle-aged man with grey hair and a round, reddish face that was known in every club, bar and restaurant in the West End. 'There are so many, you'd be surprised,' he said. 'Which particular one is interesting you at the moment?'

Mr. Budd sat down and signalled to the waitress for a coffee. 'I want ter know everythin' you can tell me about Colonel Hautboy an' The Talkin' Parrot,' he said.

Race raised his thin eyebrows. 'That's rather a tall order,' he announced. 'If I told you everything I know about The Talking Parrot, we should be here 'til next week.' He flicked a speck of dust from the coat sleeve of his immaculate grey suit. 'Can't you be more specific?'

'Have you any idea what sort o' graft goes on there?' said Mr. Budd.

'The usual at such places. You become a member, and you pay through the nose for the privilege — '

'I don't mean that, an' you know I don't,' broke in the big man. 'I mean, what goes on *be'ind*?'

'In Colonel Hautboy's expensively furnished flat?' Race shook his head. 'I can't tell you that, Budd, because I don't know.'

'An' you call yerself a gossip writer,' said Mr. Budd disgustedly.

'There's not many things I don't know, but that's one of them . . . and I'm very glad I don't,' he added.

'Why?' demanded the detective.

'I knew a man once who *did* know,' answered the gossip writer seriously. 'He came to the office of the *Sunday Telegram* and offered to sell the information to me. He wouldn't talk in the office, but made an appointment for me to go to his flat. Unfortunately, on the way home he fell in front of a train at Sloane Square Tube station and was killed. It was an accident, so they said.'

'You mean he was murdered to keep 'is mouth shut?' said Mr. Budd.

Race shrugged his shoulders. 'I'm just

telling you what happened.'

'I see,' murmured Mr. Budd thoughtfully. The waitress brought his coffee and he thanked her. 'So behind the actual club there *is* somethin' else?'

'I've always thought so,' agreed Race. He took out a packet of State Express cigarettes and selected one. 'Why have you suddenly become interested?'

'I'll tell yer, but strictly in confidence, mind,' answered Mr. Budd, and he proceeded to do so. Barry Race listened attentively.

'Well,' he commented, when the big man had finished, 'you're going to have your work cut out to hang anything on Hautboy. The man's clever and, in my opinion, dangerous. You'd better look after yourself, old man, if you cross swords with *him*.'

'You can't be clever *all* the time,' said Mr. Budd.

'Hautboy can — he *has*,' said Race quietly. 'The Talking Parrot is run impeccably. Nobody can get a drink outside the legal time for one, and nobody is admitted who isn't a member, or accompanied by a member. The place is as open and above-board as . . . as the Liberal Club. At the same time, I'm ready to wager any money that Hautboy has a finger in half the crooked deals in London.'

'Maybe 'e's near 'is Waterloo,' remarked Mr. Budd. 'I've always wanted ter pull in that feller.' He swallowed half his coffee in a single gulp.

'Roses are your favourite flowers, aren't they?' said Barry Race soberly.

Mr. Budd nodded.

'I'll send you a wreath.'

When the gossip writer had gone, Mr. Budd lingered over a second cup of coffee, thinking about the result of the interview. He was disappointed. He had expected more from Barry Race, who was usually a fount of information concerning everything and everybody within the small circle that was London's West End. It said much for Colonel Hautboy's cleverness that the gossip writer could not be more helpful.

Or, in connecting Hautboy with the death of Paula Rivers, was he on the wrong track? Maybe that very careful and slippery man had nothing to do with it at all. The membership of The Talking Parrot was large and mixed, and the proprietor could not be held responsible for the actions of all the people who belonged to the club. The person or persons who had introduced Paula Rivers there might be acting on their own. What *had* the woman found out that had necessitated her death? That was the important question. Something pretty big . . .

The superintendent finished his coffee and went back to the Yard, and when he got to his office he rang up Inspector Longfoot. Longfoot had seen the coroner, and the inquest had been fixed for ten o'clock on the following morning. It would, he told Mr. Budd, consist only of the identification and medical evidence. The police would ask for an adjournment, and the coroner had reasonably agreed not to make any objection.

The big man had just put down the receiver when Leek came in. 'There ain't no prints at all on that gun you give me,' said.

Mr. Budd grunted. 'I was afraid there wouldn't be. Maybe we'll 'ave better luck with findin' out where it was tonight.'

'It's a German pistol,' said Leek informatively. 'A Deloraine.'

'I know that,' said Mr. Budd. 'The name's engraved on the butt.'

'Oh,' muttered the sergeant, who had hoped that the information would come as a surprise. 'What about, er, ternight? I ain't got a dress suit.'

'Thank heaven fer that!' declared Mr. Budd fervently. 'I can't think of anythin' more likely ter stop us gettin' into The Talkin' Parrot than *you* in a dress suit. We're goin' as we are, openly.'

It was raining when a taxi deposited them at the unimposing entrance to The Talking Parrot just after ten o'clock that night. They passed through an arched doorway and found themselves in a square lobby with a polished counter on one side, behind which sat a uniformed attendant. From somewhere further inside they could hear the faint strains of a dance band. A silk-shaded light in the ceiling shed a soft rosy glow over everything. It was all very sedate, and very expensive.

'Good evening, gentlemen.' The man behind the counter had raised his head from a newspaper and was looking at them inquiringly.

Mr. Budd walked ponderously over to him. 'Colonel Hautboy about?' he asked.

'What name shall I say, sir?'

'Sup'n'tendent Budd an' Sergeant Leek of the Crim'nal Investigation Department, New Scotland Yard,' said Mr. Budd, and he showed his warrant card.

The receptionist's face was expressionless as he picked up the receiver of an intercommunicating telephone. 'Superintendent Budd and Sergeant Leek from New Scotland Yard to see you, sir,' he said after a pause. 'Very good, sir.' He put the telephone back on its rack. 'Colonel Hautboy will be down directly,' he announced.

They waited. In a few seconds they heard the hum of a lift, then a door opened near the other end of the lobby and a stout, bald man in immaculate evening dress came towards them.

'Good evening,' he said, with a smile that showed all his white teeth but did not reach his eyes, which were hard and wary. 'This is a pleasure. Any of the officials of Scotland Yard are always welcome at The Talking Parrot.'

'Thank you, sir,' said Mr. Budd. 'Is there any place where we could 'ave a word with you?'

'Certainly,' said Colonel Hautboy. 'I always keep a table reserved for myself and any of my friends. Come in and have a drink.'

He led the way to a curtained alcove that concealed a pair of glass swing-doors, and as he pushed them open the sound of the dance band grew suddenly louder. They descended three shallow, thickly-carpeted steps and found themselves in a fair-sized oblong room with a square of polished dance floor in the centre and a band playing on a dais at the opposite end. The dance floor was surrounded by tables and chairs, each table occupied by a small party of people, for the place was already crowded. There was a crescent-shaped bar near the entrance, behind which a man in a spotless white coat was busily mixing drinks, and in front of which lounged several men in evening dress. The air was heavy with a mixture of perfumes, and vibrant with the chattering of many voices, the shuffling of the dancers' feet, and the blare of the band. The colour scheme was subdued, with the exception of the gaudily painted parrots that adorned the walls and the numerous shades to the lamps, which had been constructed also to represent parrots. Mr. Budd noticed, as he followed Colonel Hautboy to a secluded table near the band, that only about half the people present were in evening dress.

As they sat down at the proprietor's table, a waiter came bustling up.

'What would you like, gentlemen?' asked Colonel Hautboy courteously.

'I'll 'ave some beer, if there is any,' said Mr. Budd, and Leek nervously suggested a lime juice and soda, which caused Colonel Hautboy's rather bushy eyebrows to lift slightly. He ordered the drinks, with a double Johnnie Walker for himself, and the waiter hurried away.

'Now, what can I do for you?' he asked.

'I understand,' said Mr. Budd, eyeing him sleepily, 'that you know a gal called Paula Rivers?'

'Paula Rivers?' Colonel Hautboy's brows contracted and he pursed his lips. 'Now let me see. Is she a member?'

'She may 'ave been,' said Mr. Budd. 'I wouldn't know.'

'Paula Rivers . . . ' repeated Hautboy thoughtfully.

'She was rather a pretty red-'eaded gal,' said Mr. Budd.

Hautboy looked at him quickly. '*Was?*' he said.

'She's dead,' said the big man bluntly. 'She was shot yesterday afternoon at the cinema where she worked.'

'I know the woman you're referring to *now*,' broke in Colonel Hautboy. 'She's been here once or twice. Good God! Shot, was she? What a terrible thing. How did it happen?'

'She was,' began Mr. Budd, and he broke off suddenly. His sleepy eyes had been watching over Colonel Hautboy's shoulder as the dancers shuffled round the tin floor, and he had suddenly seen a man in evening dress who was dancing with a blonde woman in a vivid scarlet frock. It was the striking patch of colour that had first attracted his attention, but it was the man who held it.

It was Mr. Foxlow, the foreman at the Mammoth Cinema!

10

Colonel Hautboy Is Not Helpful

'What's the matter?' asked Colonel Hautboy sharply. 'What are you staring at?'

'That feller ... dancin' with the woman in the red dress,' said Mr. Budd. 'Who is 'e?'

Hautboy twisted round in his chair. 'That's a man named Churchman. The woman with him is Mrs. Dacres. They often come here.'

'You're sure 'is name's Churchman?' asked Mr. Budd.

'Certainly I'm sure,' replied Hautboy in surprise. 'Why, do you know him?'

'I thought I did. But I must've been wrong.'

He was convinced that he wasn't, all the same. Unless Mr. Foxlow had a double who was as like him as two peas in a pod, the man dancing with the fair woman in scarlet was the foreman of the Mammoth Cinema.

The band finished the number it was playing at that moment, which brought the man and his partner close to the table. Colonel Hautboy, who had swung his chair round, beckoned him. 'Enjoying yourself, Mr. Churchman?' he said genially. 'My friend here seems to think that he's met you before.'

The man who was so like Foxlow regarded Mr. Budd with slightly raised brows and a hint of amusement in his eyes. 'I'm afraid he has made a mistake,' he said in a cultured voice that was completely unlike the foreman's nasal twang. 'I am sure that if we had ever met before, I should not have forgotten the occasion. I have an extraordinarily good memory.' The band started a fox-trot, and with a murmured excuse he rejoined his partner.

'Well?' inquired Colonel Hautboy.

'Remarkable,' murmured Mr. Budd, his eyes very nearly completely closed. 'I thought I might as well convince you,' said Hautboy.

'You 'ave,' replied the big man, and he spoke the truth. The man who called himself Churchman, and spoke with such a pleasant and refined accent, was one and the same with Mr. Foxlow of the uncouth speech. Mr. Budd's sleepy eyes, which missed nothing, had seen on the back of Mr. Foxlow's right hand at the Mammoth Cinema a small pear-shaped scar just below the forefinger, and the same scar was present in the same place on the right hand of Mr. Churchman.

The waiter came with their drinks. When he had gone again, Colonel Hautboy said: 'You were telling me about this woman, Paula Rivers . . . ?'

'Oh, yes, I was, wasn't I?' said Mr. Budd, jerking his mind away from the contemplation of the strange duality of Mr. Foxlow. 'Now, where was I?'

'I asked you if it was an accident,' replied Hautboy, 'that she was shot.'

'No, sir, it was no accident,' said Mr. Budd. 'She was murdered.'

'Good God! What a terrible thing. Who did it?'

'We don't know who an' we don't know why,' said Mr. Budd, shaking his head solemnly. 'That's the reason I'm 'ere ternight. I was 'oping that you might be able to 'elp me.'

'Me?' broke in Colonel Hautboy.

'You see, we're anxious to find out who introduced Miss Rivers ter this club. She was only the chief cashier at a cinema, an' she wouldn't 'ave been able to 'ave become a member of an expensive place like this on her own.'

'No, I understand what you mean,' said Hautboy. 'I'm afraid this places me in an extremely awkward position — extremely awkward.'

''Ow d'you mean?'

Colonel Hautboy drank his whisky and soda at a gulp. 'It involves a member, and naturally I do not like to involve any of my members in police inquiries. It is not good for business. The gentleman who brought Miss — er — Rivers to the club, on the few occasions that she came, is a married man and a highly respected member of the aristocracy. Anything in the nature of a scandal . . . '

'There's no reason why there should be any scandal,' interrupted Mr. Budd, 'if this gen'l'man you mention can satisfy me that 'e 'ad no 'and, directly or indirectly, with the woman's death.'

'That is unthinkable,' said Colonel Hautboy quickly.

'Nuthin's unthinkable when you're investigatin' a murder. As I was sayin' — if 'e can satisfy me that 'e 'ad nuthin' ter do with the woman's death, there need be no publicity at all.'

'Well, of course, it's my duty as a good citizen to give you his name,' said Colonel Hautboy virtuously. 'I hope, however, that you will not reveal the source of your information unless it is absolutely necessary . . . ? Thank you. The man who brought Miss Rivers here is Lord Penstemmon.'

Mr. Budd was surprised and disappointed. Lord Penstemmon was a well-known and rather impecunious peer of middle age, who had dissipated a large fortune as a young man in riotous living and was now existing on the microscopic income that had been saved from the wreck. It was very unlikely indeed that he would have been mixed up in the woman's death. The superintendent made a mental note, however, to inquire more fully into the matter.

'Is there anyone else 'ere,' said Mr. Budd, 'with whom she was friendly?'

Colonel Hautboy thought for a moment and then shook his head. 'No,' he answered. 'At least, not so far as I know. She didn't come here very frequently, as I told you; and, to be frank, I wasn't very greatly interested.'

Mr. Budd swallowed the remainder of his beer. 'D'you know a man called Figgis?' he asked suddenly.

'No,' replied Hautboy. 'I seem to have heard the name somewhere, but I have no recollection of ever having met the man. Who is he?'

'Many things,' said Mr. Budd. 'Many things. A kind of crook jack-of-all-trades.'

'A crook?' Colonel Hautboy raised his eyebrows. 'Of course, in a place like this we get all sorts of people. We do our best to keep out the undesirables, but now and again we make mistakes.'

'But not very often, I'm sure,' murmured Mr. Budd.

'No,' said Colonel Hautboy, looking him straight in the eyes, 'not very often, I hope.'

'Well, it don't seem as if you could 'elp us much,' said the big man, stifling a yawn.

'I'm afraid I can't,' agreed Hautboy regretfully. 'Won't you have another drink before you go?' he added as Mr. Budd got slowly to his feet.

'No, thank you,' said the stout superintendent. 'I've got a busy day termorrow an' I think I'd better get as much sleep as possible.'

Colonel Hautboy accompanied them to the entrance lobby. 'Come along whenever you like, Superintendent,' he said pleasantly, then turned to the man behind the reception desk. 'Harry, you're to let Superintendent Budd in whenever he comes.'

'Yes, sir,' answered Harry.

'So as to conform with the law,' said Hautboy, smiling, 'I'll make you an honorary member, Mr. Budd.'

'That's very kind of you.'

'It's a pleasure. Only too delighted.'

'Now look 'ere,' said Mr. Budd to Leek when they were outside, 'you saw that feller dancin' with the woman in red — the one what came an' spoke to us?'

'Yes,' said Leek.

'Well, you 'ang around 'ere until 'e comes out,' went on Mr. Budd rapidly, 'an' foller him. I want ter know where he lives an' as much about 'im as you can find out.'

The sergeant's melancholy face lengthened. 'It may take me the best part o' the night,' he objected.

'I don't care if it takes yer *all* night,' snarled Mr. Budd. 'That's what you're goin' to do, see?'

'All right,' said Leek resignedly. 'I'll see yer in the mornin'.'

'An' don't be late,' said Mr. Budd.

Colonel Hautboy lingered for a minute or two in the lobby after his visitors had gone, and then he took the automatic lift up to his flat. Going into the sitting-room, he locked the door and sat down at the telephone. Dialling a number, he waited, tapping impatiently with his fingers, until the connection had been made.

'Hullo,' he called softly. 'Hautboy here. The police have been in tonight making inquiries about the Rivers woman. I fobbed them off with a cock-and-bull story, but I thought I'd better let you know. No, I don't think they're on to anything. Just a routine inquiry. Rivers had kept some menus as souvenirs. Holding Figgis, are they? I didn't know *that*. Budd was asking about him. D'you think they'll get him to talk? I see. Yes, I see. Well, for God's sake be careful.'

He hung up the receiver, waited for a moment or two, and then dialled another number.

'Lord Penstemmon's residence? Is his lordship there? Tell him Colonel Hautboy wants to speak to him.' There was a pause, and then: 'That you, Penstemmon? I want you to do something for me. The police will be calling on you to ask you about a woman called Paula Rivers. *Paula Rivers*. She's dead. She was shot at the Mammoth Cinema yesterday afternoon. Don't interrupt; let me finish. I told the police that it was *you* who brought her to the club, and all you've got to do is confirm that. You won't get into any trouble at all. Now remember, the woman's name was Paula Rivers, you picked her up somewhere and took a fancy to her, and on several occasions you brought her to The Talking Parrot. I'll give you the dates — you'd better note them down and memorize them . . . I've still got that cheque, you know. I don't want to take any action about it, but of course if you force me to . . . That's all right, I was sure you wouldn't mind doing a little favour for an old friend. Now, listen. Here are the dates . . . ' He took a little book from his pocket and consulted it.

'You brought her here first on . . . ' He went carefully through half a dozen dates, repeated them, and finally rang off. Now that had been attended to, he felt better. He poured himself out a drink, lighted a cigar, and sat back in his chair smoking thoughtfully.

11

Mr. Budd Thinks Things Out

After leaving Leek outside The Talking Parrot, Mr. Budd went home to his neat house in Streatham. His housekeeper — a gaunt Scotswoman for whom he entertained a whole-hearted dread, but who looked after him like a mother — had laid a cold supper in the small dining-room before going to bed, and he did full justice to the meal, for he was hungry.

When he had finished, he went through to the kitchen and made himself a pot of tea, which he carried upstairs to his bedroom, together with milk, sugar, and cup and saucer. Returning downstairs, he bolted the front door, put out the lights, and went upstairs again. Undressing, he had a wash in the bathroom and then got into bed, arranging the pillows to form a comfortable rest for his back. Lighting one of his black cigars, he poured himself out a cup of tea and settled down to ruminate over the case of Paula Rivers.

The visit to The Talking Parrot had not been entirely without a useful result. Colonel Hautboy had not been very helpful; certainly not as helpful as he could have been if he had liked, of that the big man was sure. The air of innocence and 'wishing to do all I can' that he had adopted did not deceive Mr. Budd for a single instant. Whatever lay behind the death of Paula Rivers, Colonel Hautboy was in it — up to the neck. And that was the important thing.

What *did* lay behind it? Mr. Budd felt certain that the actual killing of Paula Rivers was a very small item in the scheme of things. She had found something out and had tried to cash in on her knowledge. What was the position *she* had occupied in the business, and what was it she had found out? What crooked game were all these people involved in — Hautboy, Figgis, and Foxlow?

The discovery of the metamorphosed foreman at The Talking Parrot had more than justified the visit to the club. There was not the slightest doubt in Mr. Budd's mind that the man called Churchman, and Foxlow, were one and the same. But why did this man, who dressed so immaculately and talked with such a cultured accent, spend the greater part of his day masquerading as an illiterate foreman of staff in a cinema? It must be in connection with the nefarious business, whatever it was, that Paula Rivers had discovered; and, that being so, it was only reasonable to suppose that part, or all, of the business was directly concerned with the Mammoth Cinema.

Mr. Budd drank his tea and poured himself out another cup. So far so good, but where could he go from here? If Hautboy was concerned with the swindle, or whatever it might be, there must be a 'big money' end to it. He wouldn't take the risk or even bother about anything small. But what could it be that involved planting one of the gang in the Mammoth Cinema? Robbery was out of the question. Mr. Budd knew enough about the routine of a cinema to know that the takings were banked each morning, and that even at the weekend, when Saturday's and Sunday's takings would be in the safe in Mr. Benstead's office until the Monday morning, there would only be a matter of three hundred or three hundred and fifty pounds at the most — much too small a sum for Hautboy to bother about. Apart from this, the dead woman had hinted that she was going to get a lot of money; and from what he had learned of Paula Rivers, a lot of money to her meant a lot of money. If she had only discovered a plot to rob the cinema, she couldn't possibly have imagined that anyone would pay her much to keep her mouth shut; and, almost certainly, they would not have gone to the length of murdering her to do so.

With robbery washed out, what remained? Mr. Budd finished his second cup of tea and cudgelled his brains, but he could think of nothing. Foxlow had been at the Mammoth Cinema for several months. What had he been doing all that time, apart from his duties a foreman? It was a decidedly puzzling business. And then there were Figgis and the old woman who whispered. What had they to do with it? The old woman had sent the warning note to Paula Rivers, and later had succeeded by a trick in getting possession of a marcasite box from the young woman's mother — a box which by some means or other had come into Paula's possession and which, according to Mrs. Rivers, she had been most anxious that no one should handle. What was the secret of this box? Did it contain something that would give a clue to the whole business? Since the mysterious old woman had taken so much trouble to get hold of it, it seemed likely.

And what about Ted Figgis? He had had a message from someone, evidently connected with The Talking Parrot, sending him to the Mammoth Cinema at the time that Paula had been shot and stating that she was no longer in danger. Mr. Budd knew perfectly well who had sent that message, and what it meant. Would a few hours in a cell have the effect of loosening his tongue, or was he too much afraid of the other people in the business with him to talk? The morrow would tell, but Mr. Budd was not very optimistic that any valuable information would be got out of Figgis. If he stuck to his story that the message had been delivered to him by mistake, it would be difficult to prove otherwise. And whatever the police might *think*, they could *do* very little without proof.

The thing that was lacking was the reason behind Paula Rivers's murder. That was the vital information that was needed. Without it, they were groping in a fog of conjecture.

Mr. Budd tried to concentrate on finding a solution to this problem, but after nearly an hour, during which he considered all kinds of suggestions that cropped up in his mind, he had to admit that he was baffled for lack of any concrete facts on which to base a theory. He put out the light and fell asleep at last without reaching any definite conclusion.

It was long past nine when he arrived at the Yard on the following morning, to find an aggrieved Leek waiting for him in his cheerless office.

'Yer tell me not to be late and then yer go an' be late yerself,' said the sergeant.

'That's different,' retorted Mr. Budd. 'I'm a sup'n'tendent an' you're a sergeant. What's the good of rank if yer can't take a few liberties? What 'ave yer got ter report on Foxlow?'

''E didn't come out o' the club until nearly two,' said Leek, 'an' then 'e walked to a big block o' flats at 'Yde Park Corner — Park Court's the name of 'em. 'E went in an' popped up in the lift. I waited a bit an' then got hold of the night porter. This feller Churchman, or whatever his name is, lives there. 'E's got a flat on the third floor — number sixty-five. I 'ung about outside an' I think I've caught a chill.'

'Never mind that,' broke in Mr. Budd impatiently. 'Did he come out again?'

The sergeant nodded. 'Yes,' he said, sniffing lugubriously. 'About four o'clock. 'E'd put on a different overcoat an' 'at — both a bit shabby — but I recognized him from 'is walk. An' a pretty dance 'e led me,' he ended bitterly. ''E walked fer miles an' miles, that feller. I don't feel as though I've got any feet left.'

'Don't worry, they're just as big as ever,' said Mr. Budd unsympathetically. 'Go on.'

'We walked all the way to Clapham,' said Leek, 'an then 'e turned down a narrow road off the 'Igh Street an' let himself into a small 'ouse with a latchkey.'

'Number Eleven, Cadby Street,' murmured Mr. Budd, consulting a list on his desk.

''Ow d'yer know that?' demanded Leek in astonishment.

'Because that's where Foxlow lodges. That's the address I've got 'ere. If I'd had any doubts before — an' I 'adn't — this clinches it. Churchman an' Foxlow wear the same 'at! What did you do then?'

'I 'ung about a bit more, an' at seven he comes out, 'ops on a bus an' gets orf at the Mammoth Cinema an' lets himself in by a side door. I 'ad some coffee an' a bit o' breakfast at a teashop an' come on 'ere.'

'You've done a good night's work,' said Mr. Budd approvingly.

'I feel worn out,' grumbled Leek. 'Me eyes is burnin' an' me legs ache an' I've got a stuffy feelin' in me 'ead.'

'You'd better go 'ome an' die peace-fully,' said Mr. Budd. 'I'll get the assistant commissioner to send a wreath.'

When Leek had gone, he rang up Inspector Longfoot and caught him just as he was leaving for the inquest. 'It's a waste of time for me ter come along,' said the superintendent. 'You can do all that's necessary. I'll be along about midday to see that feller Figgis.'

'He's raising Cain,' said the inspector. 'Talks of suing the police for damages for wrongful detention, and demands to be allowed to see his lawyer.'

'Don't let 'im see anybody,' said Mr. Budd sharply. 'I'll be there soon after twelve.'

He rang off, looked up the address of Lord Penstemmon, and set out for Chester Square. He was shown into a big room that smelt musty and looked as if it was seldom used, and after an interval of several minutes Penstemmon came in. He was a thin man with a long, weak face and thinning grey hair. His eyes were slightly red-rimmed and his hands trembled. Mr. Budd thought he looked as if he were suffering from a bad hangover.

'You wished to see me?' he inquired.

'Yes, sir,' said Mr. Budd. 'I'm sorry ter 'ave ter trouble you, but I believe you may 'ave some information that may be of assistance to the p'lice.' 'I?' Lord Penstemmon regarded him in faint surprise.

'I'm given to understand that you were acquainted with a woman called Paula Rivers. Is that right, sir?'

'Yes, yes. Now I understand,' said Penstemmon, nodding quickly. 'Poor child. She was murdered, wasn't she? I saw an account in the newspapers.'

'You *did* know her, sir?' asked Mr. Budd, and the other nodded again.

'Only slightly,' he said. 'A most attractive woman. I met her in one of the stores and took her out once or twice.'

'To The Talking Parrot, sir?'

'Yes, we went there as well as to other places. I trust,' Penstemmon added hesitantly, 'that it will not be necessary to make the fact public? My wife is rather of a jealous nature, and . . . '

'I quite understand, sir. You can rely on my discretion. Beyond just takin' her out, you knew nuthin' about 'er?'

'Nothing at all,' declared Penstemmon, shaking his head.

'Did she ever give you the impression that she was afraid of anythin'?' asked the stout superintendent.

'No. She seldom talked about herself at all.'

'I see.' Mr. Budd rubbed his fleshy chin. 'While she was with you, did she meet anybody else at The Talking Parrot, or did yer introduce her to anybody?'

'Colonel Hautboy, the proprietor, came to our table for a few minutes one evening,' replied Lord Penstemmon. 'And I introduced Miss Rivers to him, naturally.'

'She didn't know anyone else there?'

'No.'

A blank wall, thought Mr. Budd. It was impossible to believe that Penstemmon could be mixed up in Paula's death, and if he were not, then her visits to The Talking Parrot could have no bearing on it. And yet it was after that last visit that she had told her mother she expected to acquire a lot of money. There *must* be some connection.

'She didn't go to the club at any time without you, I s'pose?' he asked.

'Not to my knowledge,' said Lord Penstemmon. 'No, I'm sure she didn't. The first time she went there was with me, and she was not a member. She could not have got in.'

'Well, thank you, sir,' said Mr. Budd, concealing his disappointment. 'I'm sorry to 'ave troubled you.'

'No trouble. Sorry I can't help you. I hope you catch the person who killed her. She was a nice woman — a very nice woman.'

A sudden idea occurred to Mr. Budd, and wild as it was, he decided to put it to the test. 'And very pretty too, sir,' he murmured casually, 'if you like blondes.'

Lord Penstemmon gave a weak smile. 'All gentlemen are supposed to like blondes, aren't they?' he said, and Mr. Budd's heart gave a little jump. Paula Rivers had been a red-head! His sudden hunch had borne fruit. Lord Penstemmon had never known the woman, and therefore everything he had said had been a lie!

'Yes, sir,' he heard himself answer, 'I believe they are.'

He took his leave and walked slowly across the square. Penstemmon had lied. So had Hautboy. And, therefore, they must both be shielding the unknown person who had *really* taken Paula Rivers to The Talking Parrot.

12

Mr. Figgis Keeps His Mouth Shut

It was a little after twelve when Mr. Budd reached the police station, and Divisional Inspector Longfoot had been back from the inquest for nearly an hour.

'It was a very brief affair,' he said in reply to the stout superintendent's query. 'Just evidence of identification and the medical evidence. The coroner, at my request, has adjourned the proceedings for a fortnight.'

'Good,' grunted Mr. Budd. 'We may be able to get this thing tied up in the bag before then.'

'How did you get on at The Talking Parrot?' asked Longfoot, and the big man told him.

'I've been thinking things out,' he concluded. 'An' it's my belief that this Lord Penstemmon 'as been got at by Hautboy. I'm pretty sure 'e's never even seen Paula Rivers, much less taken 'er out. You couldn't mistake that gal fer a blonde in a month o' Sundays.'

'You think Penstemmon's in this business, whatever it is?' said the inspector.

'I didn't at first, but I do now,' said Mr. Budd. 'Let's go an' see this feller, Figgis. Maybe we can get 'im ter talk.'

The divisional inspector called for the man with keys of the cells and they went down. The cells at this station were below ground and there were six of them — three on each side of a narrow corridor. Mr. Figgis had been put in the second on the right.

'He's just had his dinner,' said the constable who accompanied them. 'He has it sent in from the eatin' house round the corner.'

He unlocked the door of the cell and they went in. Mr. Figgis was lying on the pallet bed apparently asleep, the tray with the remains of his lunch on the floor beside him.

'Wake up,' said the constable, and he shook him by the shoulder.

But Mr. Figgis did not wake up. His head rolled unpleasantly from side to side, but his eyes remained closed.

'Send for a doctor,' snapped Mr. Budd. 'The man's ill.'

The doctor came, made a brief examination, and looked at them gravely. 'This man is dead,' he said.

'Dead?' echoed the inspector. 'How did he die?'

'It looks to me as though he's been poisoned,' answered the doctor.

''Is dinner!' exclaimed Mr. Budd. 'That was it. Somebody wasn't taking any chances that he might talk.'

'But the woman from the eatin' house brought it herself, an' I took it into him, sir,' said the constable. 'There couldn't have been nothing wrong with it.'

'Send for the woman,' said Mr. Budd curtly.

While they waited for her arrival, the doctor made a closer examination of the body and gave it as his opinion that death had been due to some form of cyanide. 'The face is cyanosed,' he said, 'and there

132

is the faintest smell of almonds about the lips.' He inspected the contents of the tray. The dinner appeared to have consisted of a stew of some kind, and he sniffed at it. 'Onions,' he commented. 'That would disguise the smell if there was anything in it. However, an analysis will tell us.'

'He may have taken the stuff himself,' suggested the inspector.

'Wasn't 'e searched?' said Mr. Budd.

'Yes, but he might have succeeded in hiding a small thing like that,' said Longfoot. 'It wouldn't have taken up much room, would it, Doctor?'

The doctor shook his head. 'No,' he replied. 'It's very potent stuff. A few grains would be sufficient.'

'I don't think Figgis was the suicide type,' said Mr. Budd. 'I'm pretty certain that 'e was murdered.'

A constable came in, escorting a frightened woman of about seventeen. 'This is the woman what brought the dinner, sir,' he said stolidly.

'All right,' said Mr. Budd. 'Now, my dear,' he went on to the scared woman in his most avuncular manner, 'there's nuthin' to be frightened about. We just want to ask you a few questions, that's all.'

'Yes, sir,' she whispered nervously.

'You brought this tray, didn't yer?' said the big man, pointing to the tray on the floor of the cell.

'Yes, sir,' she said again. 'I give it to the p'liceman.'

'Who got it ready?'

'Mr. Carletta, sir.'

'Is Mr. Carletta the feller who owns the eatin' 'ouse?'

'Yes, sir.'

'When 'e'd got it ready, what did he do with it?'

''E give it ter me, sir,' said the woman, 'an' I brought it straight round 'ere.'

'Nobody could have touched it except you and Mr. Carletta, is that right?'

'Yes, sir . . . 'cept the gentleman who asked me the way ter Archford Street.'

'A gentleman asked you the way to Archford Street, eh? When was this?'

'On me way 'ere, sir. 'E stopped me an' asked me the way, an' I told 'im.'

'Did 'e do anythin' else?' demanded Mr. Budd quickly. 'Did 'e touch the tray at all?'

''E lifted the cover an' 'ad a look at the stew,' she answered. ''E said it made 'im feel 'ungry.'

'I'll bet it did,' said Mr. Budd. 'What was this feller like?'

The woman's description was vague. ''E were youngish and well-dressed' was the best she could muster. She couldn't say whether he was clean-shaven or had a moustache. She thought he had had a small one, but she wouldn't swear to it. Mr. Budd let her go and turned to Inspector Longfoot.

'That's how it was done,' he said. 'This feller dropped the stuff inter the stew when he lifted the lid. It would've been easy if 'e 'ad it concealed in the palm of his 'and. Simple but clever.'

'How did he know that Figgis would send out for his dinner?' asked the divisional inspector.

''E didn't, but it was a pretty certain bet. Anyway, it was worth tryin', and it came off.' He scratched the side of his face thoughtfully. 'They must've been pretty afraid of what 'e'd say if he talked,' he remarked. 'Get 'im to the mortuary an' 'ave the remains o' that stew analysed. I'm goin' along ter the Mammoth Cinema.'

The cinema had just opened when he arrived; and the first person he saw, standing at the front in his ill-fitting uniform, was Mr. Foxlow. It was impossible to believe that this man was the same immaculate individual he had seen dancing at The Talking Parrot on the previous night.

'Good mornin',' said the superintendent.

'Good *afternoon*, sir,' corrected the foreman. 'Mr. Benstead h'is 'avin' lunch h'in the café.'

'Let him finish it,' said Mr. Budd. 'Were you busy yesterday?'

'Yesterday was me day orf,' answered Mr. Foxlow.

'Oh, I see,' murmured Mr. Budd. 'What d'yer usually do on yer day orf?'

'Well, h'it depends. H'if it's fine I goes fer a bit of a walk, an' h'if it's wet I stays at 'ome an' 'as a read. I'm rather partial to a good thriller.'

'You don't go dancing, by any chance?'

'Dancin'?' Mr. Foxlow sniffed disparagingly. 'Not me. I don't 'old with h'all this dancin' an' skedaddlin' about. Jitterbuggin' and jivin', or whatever they calls it. H'all very well fer a lot o' 'eathens, that's what I say.'

'It seems pretty popular,' said Mr. Budd. 'I was at a place called The Talkin' Parrot last night an' it was full.'

'The Talkin' Parrot? That's a queer name, that is. What sort of a place h'is that?'

'It's a nightclub. Paula Rivers went there several times.'

'Did she, now?' said Mr. Foxlow with sudden interest. 'I can well believe *that*. H'if yer ask me, there'd be a lot less trouble h'if them sort o' places was h'all shut down. I wonder the p'lice don't do somethin' about that.'

'Maybe they'd like to. But so long as these places keep within the law, they're powerless to act.'

'Then the law should be h'altered,'

affirmed Mr. Foxlow. 'Ave you found out anythin' about the killin' o' that poor gal?' 'Quite a bit,' replied Mr. Budd.

'A terrible thing to 'ave 'appened,' said the foreman, shaking his head. 'Though I 'spect she arst fer it. Flighty bit o' goods, like most o' these 'ere gals nowadays. Still, whoever done it ought ter get hung.'

'They will be,' said Mr. Budd. 'That's as certain as termorrer mornin'.'

'I'm glad to 'ear yer say so,' said Mr. Foxlow. 'Good h'afternoon, sir.' Harry Stanton, the organist, had come out of the cinema and approached them.

'Is Mr. Benstead up in the café, Foxlow?' Stanton asked, nodding to Mr. Budd.

''Avin' his lunch,' said the foreman.

'I'll join him, then. How are things progressing, Superintendent?'

'Not too badly, sir,' answered Mr. Budd.

'Poor little Paula,' said Stanton, shaking his head. 'She was a silly woman in lots of ways, but she didn't deserve *that*. I wonder why she was killed.'

'That,' said Mr. Budd, 'is somethin' I

should very much like to know, sir.'

'Well, I hope you find out,' said Stanton. 'So long.' He went up the steps to the circle two at a time and disappeared into the cafe.

'Nice feller,' said Mr. Budd. 'Well, I must be goin'. I've got to get ter 'Yde Park Corner ter see a man what lives in Park Court — a feller called Churchman. D'yer know him?'

'I can't say that I do,' said Mr. Foxlow seriously. ''E wouldn't be the chap what makes them cigarettes, would 'e?' he added innocently.

'No,' answered Mr. Budd, ''e wouldn't.'

13

The Metamorphosis of Eileen

Jimmy Redfern had to wait two days before he could see George Nicholls. He rang him up only to be told that he was away; and then on the morning of the third day, the big Lagonda swung into the garage where Jimmy worked and Nicholls jumped out. 'Fill her up, Redfern, will you?' he said pleasantly.

'Yes, Mr. Nicholls,' answered Jimmy. 'I've been trying to get in touch with you.'

'Have you?' said Nicholls, lighting a cigarette and holding out his case. 'I've been in the country — only just got back. What's it all about?'

Jimmy told him, and George Nicholls's cheery round face showed his interest. 'Want me to take you and this woman to The Talking Parrot, eh?' he said when Jimmy had finished the whole story.

'I'll pay all expenses,' began Jimmy, but

Nicholls cut him short.

'Never mind that, and you won't do anything of the sort,' he declared. 'I'm grateful to be let in on this. Always rather fancied myself in the role of the great detective. By Jove, if we could find anything out it would be a great lark! When do you want to go?'

'Whenever you like.'

'What about tonight?' suggested Nicholls after a moment's thought.

'That suits me,' said Jimmy. 'I'll get in touch with Eileen at once.'

'O.K. Meet you with the car outside the Tube station at nine-twenty. How's that?'

'Fine. It's very decent of you, Mr. Nicholls.'

'Nonsense,' said Nicholls, waving away his thanks. 'I'm looking forward to it. I'd like to get one over on that fellow Hautboy. He threatened to have me thrown out of his wretched club once.'

When he had gone Jimmy Redfern got through to the shop where Eileen worked and told her.

'Jimmy, that's wonderful,' she said.

'You'd better call for me at our house around nine.'

Jimmy Redfern took a long time dressing that evening. He had a nearly new dinner suit which he had originally bought to take Paula out, but which he had scarcely worn when she had begun to make more and more excuses for not meeting him. When he had shaved and had a bath he put this on, surveying the result critically in the mirror. The suit had been well cut and fitted him perfectly. He decided that even at such a smart place as The Talking Parrot, he would pass muster. The thing that worried him a little was Eileen. What was she going to look like? She always appeared so colourless and drab. He rather wished that he had given her a hint over the telephone to smarten herself up as much as possible. If it had been Paula, he thought with the stab of a painful memory, there would have been no need to worry. She always looked lovely. But Eileen . . . He set out for Eden Street in great trepidation.

Mrs. Rivers opened the door in answer to his knock. She looked very lined and old, and the traces of her grief were still visible. In some queer way, he thought, she seemed to have shrunk.

'Come in, Jimmy,' she said, conjuring up a faint smile. 'Eileen's just finishing dressing. She'll be down in a minute.'

He followed her through into the kitchen, remembering avidly how many times in the old days he had called for Paula and been greeted with almost the same words.

'It'll do Eileen good to go out,' said Mrs. Rivers. 'I've always told her she don't go out enough . . . Not like Paula.' He saw the tears gather in her eyes.

'Did Eileen tell you where we were going?' he asked hastily.

'Yes; though I don't see that much good can come of it — finding out anything about Paula, I mean. That's what the p'lice are for, and if *they* can't . . . '

'The majority of the police are known to these places,' explained Jimmy. 'We may pick up something, or hear something, because they won't suspect us.'

'Well, I do hope you won't get into any

trouble,' said Mrs. Rivers anxiously. 'There's been trouble enough already, goodness knows.'

'We shall be all right, Mother,' broke in Eileen's voice. 'I'm not late, Jimmy. You're ten minutes early.'

He turned and — stared! This couldn't be Eileen — this lovely woman who stood smiling at him in the open doorway. There was a sheen on her pale, honey-coloured hair that was like a nimbus about her head, and her shining eyes were shaded by long dark lashes. She was dressed in a long gown of soft black chiffon that was moulded skin-tight round her hips, and from the close-fitting bodice of which her neck and shoulders rose a warm cream. She wore a spray of red roses that matched the colour of her lips exactly.

Colourless? Drab? Jimmy Redfern felt the blood come into his cheeks as he remembered. This woman was beautiful, with a delicate and refined beauty that the flamboyant Paula had never possessed.

She saw the admiration come into his

eyes and her face flushed softly. 'Will I do?' she asked.

'You look lovely,' he answered.

'I've never seen you look so nice, Eileen,' said Mrs. Rivers. 'Surely that's a new dress?'

'Yes, Mother. I bought it yesterday. Do you like my hair? I had it done at Semmons.'

'You look very nice altogether,' said her mother, and sighed. 'Paula would have thought so, too,' she added tearfully.

'We'd better be going,' said Jimmy, sensing that there might be a scene imminent.

'I'll get my coat,' said Eileen. 'I borrowed *that* from Margaret at the shop.' She ran quickly up the stairs and was back in a few seconds with a mink coat round her shoulders. 'You're sure you'll be all right, Mother?' she said as she kissed her.

'Yes, dear,' said Mrs. Rivers. 'I shall go to bed as soon as you've gone. Do be careful, won't you?'

They both reassured her and went out into the semi-darkness of Eden Street.

'I *do* feel excited,' said Eileen, resting her hand on Jimmy's arm. 'Do you think we shall discover anything?'

'Maybe not this time,' he answered. 'It would be a bit too much to expect.' 'How many times are we going, then?'

'As many as we can. I'm sure that the secret of Paula's murder is at The Talking Parrot, and we're going to find it out.'

The big Lagonda was waiting outside the tube station when they got there, and Jimmy introduced Eileen to George Nicholls. That cheery-faced man was obviously both impressed and surprised.

'It's very good of you to take all this trouble, Mr. Nicholls,' said Eileen as the car sped swiftly westwards.

'It's a pleasure,' said Nicholls, and he sounded as if he really meant it. 'And, look here — suppose we drop the 'Mr. Nicholls', eh? My name's George.'

'All right, George,' agreed Eileen. She was feeling so completely happy that she would have agreed to anything at that moment. This was the first time she had ever been out with Jimmy Redfern, and even the fact that it was a semi-business trip and they were engaged on a serious investigation did not detract from her pleasure.

The receptionist at The Talking Parrot greeted Nicholls like an old friend. 'Good evening, sir,' he said. 'You haven't been here for some time.'

'Can't be everywhere, Harry,' said Nicholls, scribbling his name in the big ledger. 'How's things?'

'About as usual, sir,' answered Harry. 'You'll find it a bit full tonight.'

Nicholls nodded and led the way over to the swing doors. The place was full. Nearly every table was occupied, and the dance floor was so congested that the dancers looked almost like a solid mass.

'By Jove,' said Nicholls as they stood at the foot of the steps and looked about them, 'he was right. I've never seen so many people here before.'

The head waiter came forward, smiling. 'Good evening, Mr. Nicholls. You want a table?'

'Can you find one, Emile?' asked Nicholls.

'For you, sir, always. This way, please.'

He threaded his way deftly through the tables and they followed closely behind him. Near the band dais was a table with an 'engaged' card propped up against the flower vase. Emile whisked it away and pulled out a chair for Eileen, with a bow.

'We always keep one or two tables reserved for unexpected patrons, sir,' he said, smiling at Nicholls. 'I will send a waiter to take your order.'

'So this is a nightclub,' remarked Eileen, gazing interestedly about her.

'Haven't you ever been to one before?' asked Nicholls.

She shook her head and let her coat slip from her shoulders. 'No. My education has been sadly neglected.'

'I think you should regard it as an asset,' he replied, looking at her admiringly. 'The educational value of nightclubs is not of a very high standard.'

A waiter came hurriedly over to the table, and Nicholls ordered drinks. 'Shall we dance?' he asked as the band struck up a quickstep. Eileen nodded.

Jimmy Redfern watched them mingle

with the crowd on the dance floor, and he was surprised that he felt a little annoyed. They stayed for the slow foxtrot, which followed the quickstep, and came back laughing. Eileen's eyes were sparkling and she looked radiant, and Jimmy noticed that quite a large percentage of the men present were watching her.

'That was nice,' she said, sipping her gin and orange. 'I think.'

Emile came quickly up to their table. 'Excuse me — Miss Eileen Rivers?'

'Yes?' she said in surprise.

'You are wanted on the telephone, miss.'

'Me?' Her eyes went wide with astonishment. 'How could anybody know I'm here?'

'How did *you* know this was Miss Rivers?' asked Jimmy Redfern suspiciously.

The head waiter smiled. 'The caller asked to speak to Miss Eileen Rivers, the lady who was with Mr. Nicholls, sir,' he explained. 'The telephone is in the lobby, miss,' he added.

Eileen rose. 'I'd better see who it is,'

she said with a puzzled frown. 'I won't be a minute.'

The telephone cabinet was close beside the reception counter, and the man, Harry, signed to her to go in. 'I'll switch you through, miss,' he said.

She went in, closed the glass door, and picked up the receiver. 'Hello?' she called.

'Miss Eileen Rivers?' asked a voice in a queer husky whisper that made her heart give a sudden jump.

'Yes,' she murmured. 'Who . . . ?'

'Go home!' said the whispering voice urgently. 'Get out of this place at once!'

'But — ' she began.

'Do as I tell you,' croaked the voice. 'I warned your sister, and you know what happened to her. Do you want the same thing to happen to you? Get out before it's too late.' There was a click and the line went dead. The whispering woman had rung off.

14

Colonel Hautboy Is Perturbed

Colonel Hautboy carefully poured himself out a double whisky from the bottle of Johnny Walker on the silver tray by his side, squirted in a little soda, and held the glass up to the light to watch the bubbles. He had just had a hot bath and was comfortably clad in a flowery silk dressing-gown. The Talking Parrot had seen all that it was going to see of him that night. He drank half his drink and lighted a cigar, leaning back in the deep armchair, at peace with the world.

And then the telephone bell rang. Colonel Hautboy growled an oath. For a second or two he contemplated letting it ring, and then decided that it might be important. Going over, he lifted the receiver. At the first sound of the voice that came over the wire, he realized that it was important.

'Paula Rivers's sister is in the club,' it said. 'She came with Redfern and a man called Nicholls. Be careful.'

'What do you want me to do?' asked Hautboy.

'Watch her,' came the answer curtly. 'She may know something — her sister may have told her something. We can't afford to take risks.'

'All right. I'll see to it.'

'Who is this man Nicholls?'

'An old member of the club; used to come here quite a lot and pretty regularly. Heaps of money.'

'Find out how he got to know the Rivers woman and Redfern. Any news for me?'

'No. Everything's all right at this end.'

'See that it remains so. I'm keeping away for a bit — until the Paula business dies down a little, anyway. I think it's safer. I'll keep in touch with you by phone.'

'Where can I get hold of you in case of emergency?'

'You can't. I'll ring you morning and evening.' He hung up before Hautboy could reply. For a few seconds he stood with the receiver still in his hand, thinking, with a frown on his face. Then he put it back on the rack and went over and drank the remainder of his whisky. Putting down his cigar in the ashtray, he went into his bedroom and began to dress. Ten minutes later he was descending to the club in his private lift.

Harry, the receptionist, looked at him in surprise as he emerged into the lobby. 'Thought you weren't coming down any more tonight, guv'nor?' he said.

'I thought so, too,' grunted Hautboy. 'Mr. Nicholls is inside, isn't he?'

Harry nodded. 'Yes, with two guests,' he answered. 'One of 'em's the sister of that woman who was killed — a smashing piece of goods!'

'I know,' said Hautboy.

'She had a telephone call a few minutes ago. Someone with a queer sort of voice, as if they had a bad cold.'

'A woman, was it?' asked Colonel Hautboy sharply.

'You couldn't tell. It's a funny thing, but you can't tell the sex or anything of a whisper over the telephone. Have you ever noticed that, guv'nor?'

'No,' said Hautboy, 'but I'll take your word for it.' He fingered his white tie thoughtfully. 'Did you hear anything this . . . person said?'

'No,' replied the receptionist, shaking his head.

Colonel Hautboy walked away and pushed open the swing doors leading into the club. The newspapers had been full of a mysterious old woman with a whispering voice who had sent a warning letter to the dead woman by her sister. The police had been looking for her, and a description had been circulated. Was it she who had rung up Eileen Rivers at The Talking Parrot? And if so, who was she, and how did she know so much? Hautboy felt vaguely uneasy and perturbed as he made his way around the tables, nodding and smiling to the various people he knew.

George Nicholls was sitting alone when he reached that particular table. 'Good evening, Nicholls,' he said. 'Glad to see you here tonight. It's quite a while since you were here last.'

''Lo, Hautboy,' said George. 'Thought you weren't on view tonight.'

'I'm more or less always on view. Are you alone?'

'No, I've got a couple of people with me — Miss Rivers and Mr. Redfern.'

'Miss Rivers?' Colonel Hautboy's brows rose slightly. 'That's the name of that poor woman who was murdered in the cinema the other day. She came here once or twice.'

'This is her sister. Redfern was engaged to the woman who was killed — Paula.'

'Indeed? Rather strange to come to a place like this so soon after the — er — tragedy, isn't it?'

'They heard that Paula had been here and they wanted to see what it was like,' answered Nicholls.

'I hope their — curiosity — is satisfied. Here they are, I think. Perhaps you will introduce me?'

The band had finished playing, and Eileen and Jimmy came back to their table.

'This is Colonel Hautboy, the owner of

the club,' said George. 'Miss Rivers . . . Mr. Redfern . . . '

'Very pleased to welcome you to The Talking Parrot,' said Hautboy genially. 'I hope you are enjoying yourselves?'

'*I* am,' answered Eileen, and Jimmy Redfern nodded shortly.

'That's right,' Hautboy continued. 'We like the people who come here to enjoy themselves.'

'Did Paula enjoy herself?' asked Jimmy curtly.

'Yes, on the few occasions she came here I think she did,' replied Colonel Hautboy, completely unperturbed by the abruptness of the question. 'You were, I believe, engaged to her?'

'More or less,' said Jimmy. He had taken an almost instant dislike to this sleek, well-dressed man who showed so many teeth when he smiled.

'May I be permitted to offer my sympathy?' said Colonel Hautboy, lowering his voice. 'When I heard about Miss Rivers's tragic death, I was appalled.'

'Thank you,' said Jimmy. 'I'm sure you must have been.'

'It came as all the more of a shock to me because she was here the night before,' continued Colonel Hautboy. 'The last time I saw her, she was dancing with Lord Penstemmon.'

'That old bounder?' interjected Nicholls. 'How did *he* get hold of her?'

'It was Lord Penstemmon who introduced Miss Rivers to the club,' said Hautboy glibly. 'How he became acquainted with her, I have no idea.'

'Who is Lord Penstemmon?' asked Eileen curiously.

'A middle-aged old roué who's run through a fortune in riotous living and is now practically dead broke,' answered Nicholls bluntly.

'Really, Mr. Nicholls,' protested Colonel Hautboy, 'I don't think you should — '

'It's the truth and you know it,' interrupted Nicholls. 'Everybody in this set knows it!'

'Well, Lord Penstemmon is certainly not as rich as he was,' said Hautboy cautiously, 'but . . . '

'You say *he* brought Paula here?' asked Eileen.

Hautboy nodded. 'Yes, Miss Rivers,' he answered. 'On the few occasions when she came to the club, she was with Lord Penstemmon.'

Emile came up deferentially and whispered in Hautboy's ear. 'Excuse me,' the proprietor said hastily. 'Something has happened that requires my immediate attention.' He went away with the head waiter, and Jimmy Redfern looked at Eileen.

'Well,' he remarked, 'we've found out something. We know who brought Paula to The Talking Parrot.'

She nodded slowly, her brows puckered in a frown. 'I wonder why?' she said. 'George, you know the man. Could he have had anything to do with ... with ... ?'

'I shouldn't think so,' said George Nicholls. 'Penstemmon is capable of most things, but he wouldn't get mixed up with murder.'

'I don't like that fellow Hautboy,' said Jimmy bluntly. 'There's something slimy about him.'

'I don't like him either,' said Nicholls.

'I never have liked him.'

'We don't seem to be getting very far, do we?' put in Eileen. 'If Paula came here with Lord Penstemmon, and you don't think he could be connected with her death, then it looks as if we were wrong in thinking that this place was.'

'Oh, I don't know,' said Jimmy. 'She may have come with Penstemmon, but it's quite possible she met somebody else here.'

'There's Penstemmon now,' broke in Nicholls suddenly. 'Just come in.'

They turned and looked toward the entrance. Lord Penstemmon was standing by the bar, staring rather vacantly about as though in search of someone.

'I don't like the look of him, anyhow,' said Eileen candidly.

'Neither do I,' agreed Jimmy. 'Look, there's Hautboy.'

Colonel Hautboy came hurriedly through the swing doors from the lobby, went up to Penstemmon and began speaking rapidly and, to judge from his expression, urgently. Penstemmon appeared to be a little annoyed. He shook his head and his weak mouth set obstinately. Hautboy's manner became even more urgent. Finally he caught hold of the other's arm and almost dragged him up the shallow steps and through the swing doors.

'What do you make of that?' asked Jimmy. 'It looks as though his lordship wasn't welcome.'

'More likely they've decided not to grant him any more credit,' said Nicholls. 'I believe he's run up bills all over London.'

'Or perhaps,' suggested Eileen, 'Colonel Hautboy doesn't want *us* to meet him!'

'I never thought of that,' said Jimmy, 'but I believe you've hit on it. In which case, there is something that Penstemmon knows about Paula.'

'Here's Hautboy back again,' said Nicholls. 'Not too good-tempered, either, by the look of him.'

'He's coming over here,' murmured Jimmy.

Colonel Hautboy came quickly up to their table, and by the time he reached it his face had cleared. 'Sorry I had to run away like that,' he apologized. 'Somebody wanted a cheque cashed.'

'Wasn't that old Penstemmon who came in just now?' asked Nicholls.

Hautboy nodded. 'Yes,' he answered. 'He was looking for a friend.'

'He didn't look very long,' said Jimmy.

'No,' said Hautboy, smiling. 'He remembered that it wasn't here that he'd arranged to meet her after all. Silly mistake, wasn't it?'

'Very silly,' said Jimmy in a tone that was so obviously disbelieving that Hautboy glanced at him sharply.

'I'm afraid Penstemmon is a trifle absent-minded about most things,' he said. 'One of these days . . . ' He broke off as a waiter came up with a package on a tray.

'This has just been left for you, sir,' he said.

'For me?' Colonel Hautboy frowned.

'Yes, sir, at the reception desk. The person who left it said that it was urgent you should have it.'

Colonel Hautboy picked up the little

package, looked at it, weighed it, and ripped off the brown paper covering. 'Excuse me . . . ' he began, and stopped abruptly as he saw the small object it had concealed.

'Why,' exclaimed Eileen in amazed wonder, 'that belonged to Paula!'

Colonel Hautboy said nothing, but his face was grey as he stared at the marcasite box in the palm of his hand.

15

Mr. Foxlow Receives a Visitor

Colonel Hautboy recovered himself quickly. 'I'm afraid you're mistaken, Miss Rivers,' he said easily. 'Your sister may have had a little box *like* this, but I assure you this was never in her possession. There are many of them about.' He slipped the box into his pocket.

Eileen looked at Jimmy, and on his face she saw a disbelief as great as her own. Hautboy was lying. The marcasite box in his pocket *was* the one Paula had almost snatched out of her mother's hand on the last morning she had been alive. For a fraction of a second the mask had dropped, and she had seen the consternation and dismay behind it. And the box had been secured by a trick on the part of the shabby old woman in black. Why had it been sent to Colonel Hautboy? Short of openly declaring him to be a liar, she was forced to accept his denial that it had belonged to Paula, but she was quite certain all the same.

Hautboy sensed this disbelief and tried to dispel it. 'It's a useful little thing to keep one's studs and links in,' he said. 'I asked a friend of mine to get it for me. You say your sister had one like it, Miss Rivers?'

'Yes,' answered Eileen, looking at him steadily. *'Exactly like it.'*

'Curious,' he murmured. 'Well, I'm afraid I've got a lot of work to do, so I'll say good night. I hope you'll both come again, any time you wish to. Just ask for me and I shall be pleased to sign you in — as my guests, of course. Good night, Nicholls.' He nodded and walked hurriedly away.

When he reached the lobby, he went straight up to the reception desk. 'Who brought that little packet for me?' he asked harshly.

'A queer old woman in black,' said Harry. 'Just like a witch, she was.'

'Did she say anything?'

'Only that it was for you and that it was urgent. Funny voice she had. Husky, like a loud whisper.'

'I'm going up to my flat,' said Hautboy abruptly. 'I'm not to be disturbed. Emile can deal with anything that turns up. You understand?'

Harry nodded and Hautboy went over to the lift, stepped inside and was carried rapidly upwards. He was a greatly perturbed and puzzled man — more than a little scared, too. Again he asked himself who this mysterious old woman was who seemed to know so much.

He went into his bedroom, changed into a dressing-gown, and coming back into the sitting-room poured himself out four fingers of Johnny Walker, which he drank neat at a gulp. He had brought the marcasite box with him and now he examined it carefully.

It was quite empty. He frowned, staring at it in the palm of his hand. If, as her sister said, it had been in Paula Rivers's possession, how had it come into the possession of the old woman with the whispering voice? And why had she brought it to him? The latter question was easily answered. She wanted him to realize that she knew its significance. And if she knew that, she must know a great deal more — and the knowledge was likely to prove dangerous.

Colonel Hautboy took a silk handkerchief from his pocket and wiped his suddenly damp forehead. The police were searching for her. If they found her and she talked . . . He felt a little shiver at the possibility of such a calamity, for it would be nothing else. Something ought to be done to ensure that such a thing could not happen — but what?

He lighted a cigar and began to pace up and down, smoking jerkily. Who the devil was this woman, and what game was she playing? If she knew as much as it appeared she did, why didn't she go to the police? There must be some reason for that. Perhaps there was a very good reason. Perhaps she *dare* not. He tried to comfort himself with this belief, but it didn't help a great deal towards eradicating the fears that were destroying his peace of mind.

★   ★   ★

Mr. Foxlow changed slowly from his ill-fitting uniform to the blue and equally ill-fitting suit that clothed him during a portion of his leisure hours. The feature picture was two-thirds of the way through its last screening, and in another half an hour the Mammoth Cinema would be closing its doors for the night. Mr. Foxlow realized the fact with relief. He came out of the men's staffroom, strolled along the narrow gangway at the back of the circle, and made his way down to the lower vestibule.

Grace Singer came out of the manager's office with the envelope containing the daily returns, sealed and stamped ready for dispatch to the head office. She looked tired.

'Will you have this posted, Mr. Foxlow?' she said wearily.

The foreman nodded and called to King. ''Ere, take this ter the post,' he said, and the attendant took the envelope and hurried out. 'Got double work ter do now, ain't yer?' he said to the woman.

'Yes, until they get another cashier,' she answered. 'Mr. Benstead's got someone coming for an interview tomorrow. I'm going to take Paula's place though as first cashier.'

'So yer ought,' said Mr. Foxlow decidedly. 'That's h'only fair, ain't it? Not that it means more'n a bob or two extra, I s'pose. Still, every little 'elps, don't it?'

Grace nodded. 'I suppose so,' she said. 'Good night.'

She went slowly up the stairs to the circle to get her coat from the women's staffroom, a drooping, rather despondent figure.

Mr. Foxlow watched her until she was out of sight, shook his head for some reason best known to himself, and set to work to carry out such odd duties as would fill in the time until he could leave.

He was, as usual, the last out of the cinema, leaving by the side door to which he had a key. The door opened onto a narrow alley that ran the length of the building and was bordered on the other side by a high brick wall forming one side of a tall block of offices.

A man who had been lurking in the shadows at the other end of this alley saw the figure of the foreman leave the cinema and followed in his wake, taking care to keep a respectful distance behind him. If Mr. Foxlow had any knowledge of the presence of the trailer, he gave no sign of it. Without looking back, he hurried down the main street until he reached the junction. To get to Cadby Street he should have turned left here, but apparently he had no intention of going to his lodgings, for he took the right-hand road, walked briskly along it for a hundred yards and then turned into a side street. Halfway down this was a lock-up garage to which Mr. Foxlow admitted himself with a key.

The watcher hung about in a doorway on the opposite side of the narrow street and waited. Presently a long black Rolls nosed slowly out of the garage, stopped, and Mr. Foxlow got out and locked the door. Then he got back into the driving seat and sent the big car speeding up the street.

The man in the doorway watched it

disappear in the darkness, and then he emerged from his shelter and hurried away in search of the nearest public call office.

Mr. Foxlow reached Hyde Park Corner just before midnight. He drove into the forecourt of the big block of flats in which Mr. Churchman resided, and when he got out of the car he was wearing a smart overcoat over his shabby blue suit.

The night porter touched his hat as Mr. Foxlow made his way across the vestibule to the lift and watched disinterestedly as he pulled back the grille and stepped inside. He was used to the erratic coming and going of Mr. Churchman, who was a gentleman of gregarious habits, but a very pleasant gentleman all the same.

Mr. Foxlow let himself into Mr. Churchman's flat, discarded his overcoat, and, going through into the bathroom, turned on the hot-water tap. While the bath was filling, he undressed, and, clad in a dressing-gown, drank a large whisky and soda with great enjoyment. He retired to the bathroom and presently emerged a completely different personality. The physical characteristics of Mr. Foxlow, foreman of the Mammoth Cinema, remained, but the man who poured himself out another drink and drank it slowly while he thoughtfully smoked a cigarette was the man who had danced with the woman in the scarlet dress at The Talking Parrot. The difference was subtle but unmistakable. All that had made up the personality of Mr. Foxlow had vanished and been replaced by the cultured Mr. Churchman.

He went over to a large pedestal desk, sat down in a swivel chair, and, unlocking a drawer, produced some papers which he studied carefully. So absorbed did he become in these documents that he failed to hear a slight noise that came from the passage outside the closed door of the room. It was the vaguest of sounds — as though something soft had brushed for a moment against the wall; and then everything was silent again. The door moved slightly and began to open.

'Keep still, my friend,' said a muffled voice, and the man at the desk started and looked up. Partially concealed by the half-open door was a figure in a long mackintosh, holding in one gloved hand a stubby automatic that was pointed steadily at Mr. Churchman.

'Don't move,' went on the muffled voice. 'I don't want to pull the trigger of this thing, but if you move I shall be compelled to.'

'What do you want?' asked Mr. Churchman calmly.

'I want an answer to a simple question,' said the man at the door, and he came a foot further into the room. The reason for the muffled effect to his voice was now visible. A dark scarf covered the lower half of his face. 'Who are you?'

'The porter could have told you that,' said Churchman coolly.

'Could he?' retorted the visitor. 'You call yourself Churchman here and Foxlow at the Mammoth Cinema, where you work as chief of staff. Who are you, really?'

'A man in his time plays many parts,' began Churchman.

'I'm serious,' snapped the other harshly.

'This is anything but a joke, I assure you!'

'I am under no misapprehension about that,' said Churchman steadily.

'Then tell me the truth. What's your game?'

'What's yours?' demanded Churchman. He was playing for time, hoping that his wits would supply him with a way out of this unpleasant and dangerous predicament.

It seemed as if the visitor read his thoughts, for he said curtly: 'Don't quibble. I'll give you two minutes to answer my question.'

'And then?'

The other didn't answer, but the movement he made with the pistol was sufficient.

'Well, I suppose I'd better tell you,' went on Churchman. 'The fact is . . . ' His foot shot out suddenly and a wooden waste-paper basket beside the desk went hurtling towards the man at the door. He fired, but at the same instant Churchman flung himself forward and the bullet whined over his head. Before the intruder could fire again, the heavy waste-paper basket struck him full on the chest and made him stagger. Churchman was on his feet in a second and brought him down with a flying tackle that would have been greeted with joy on a rugby field.

'Now,' he panted, gripping the other's pistol wrist and smashing his knuckles against the edge of the door, 'I'm going to have a look at you.'

The man uttered a howl of pain and the automatic flew out of his hand. Churchman made a grab for it — and that was his mistake; for the other, taking advantage of the momentary slackening of his grasp, hoisted himself free and leapt to his feet. Before Churchman could follow suit, he was out of the door and along the passage. He wrenched open the front door and Churchman heard him utter a startled cry, which was immediately followed by a gasping grunt and the sound of a heavy fall. Churchman tore along the hall and nearly fell headlong over the body of a man that sprawled across the threshold.

'What the 'ell's goin' on here?'

174

demanded a breathless voice, and the body heaved itself up and glared wrathfully at Churchman. It was Mr. Budd!

16

Mr. Churchman Explains

The big man hauled himself gingerly to his feet and rubbed delicately at those portions of his anatomy that had come in violent contact with the hard floor.

'What's goin' on 'ere?' he grunted again. 'D'you know I could charge you with assaultin' an officer of the law in the execution of 'is duty?'

'You couldn't,' said Churchman, 'because it wasn't me. What were you doing outside my door at this hour of the night, anyhow?'

'I was just goin' ter ring the bell,' answered Mr. Budd truthfully. 'Who's the feller who came bargin' out an' knocked me over?'

Mr. Churchman shook his head. 'I'd like to know that,' he said. 'I never got a chance to see his face.' He thought for a moment. 'If you were coming to see me, you'd better come in. I'm going to have a drink, and I should think you could do with one, too.'

He led the way to the sitting-room and Mr. Budd followed him. In silence he poured out two stiff whiskies from the bottle of Johnny Walker and handed one to the big man. 'I'd sooner 'ave beer,' remarked Mr. Budd.

'This'll do you more good,' said Churchman. He swallowed half his whisky, set the glass down and helped himself to a cigarette. 'What brought you here?'

Mr. Budd took a mouthful of whisky and allowed it to trickle slowly down his throat. When it was gone, he smacked his lips and took another. 'Good stuff, that,' he remarked, gazing into the half-empty glass dreamily.

'Don't you think you'd better do a bit of explaining?' suggested Churchman. 'Who are you?'

'You know very well who I am,' said Mr. Budd.

'Do I?' Churchman raised his eye-brows.

'We met at The Talkin' Parrot. Remember?'

'Of course.' The other nodded. 'Now that you remind me, I recollect the occasion.'

'And we've met a good many times apart from that. At the Mammoth Cinema.'

'Really?' Churchman inhaled deeply and blew out a thin stream of smoke. 'I don't think I remember *that* . . . '

'It isn't me that's got to do the explainin',' went on Mr. Budd. '*You've* got ter do that, you know.'

'Why?'

'Because this isn't a game. This is a murder investigation!'

Churchman's face changed, and when he spoke the faint bantering note had left his voice. 'You're quite right,' he said seriously. 'It isn't a game at all. It's wicked and diabolical.'

Mr. Budd swallowed the remainder of his whisky and put down the empty glass. 'Look 'ere,' he said, 'I'll be candid with yer. It's no use you tryin' to pretend you ain't Foxlow. I've had you tailed.'

'Most interesting. Very well, I'll be equally candid. I *am* Foxlow.'

'That's better,' said the big man, nodding approvingly. 'Now we know where we are. P'raps you'll go a bit further an' tell me why.'

'Have another drink?' suggested Churchman, picking up the bottle of Johnny Walker.

'Thank you, I don't mind a small one.'

Churchman poured whisky into his own and the other's glass. 'It's a long story,' he said, giving the glass to Mr. Budd. 'You'd better sit down and make yourself comfortable.'

The stout superintendent lowered himself carefully into a big chair and rested the glass on his broad knee. Through half-closed lids he watched Churchman as he stood frowning at the glass in his hand.

'I suppose you know,' he began suddenly, 'that during the past eighteen months there has been a very considerable increase in the drugs traffic?'

Mr. Budd's eyes opened quickly and widely. 'So *that's* it?' he remarked.

Churchman nodded. 'That's it, in a nutshell. There has been a sharp rise in the number of drug addicts throughout the country, and particularly in London. Somebody has been very cleverly smuggling vast quantities of cocaine, heroin, opium and other illicit drugs into the country and distributing them with equal cleverness. This organization — for there is no doubt that a considerable number of people are involved — has been, and is, operating on a huge scale, far bigger than anything of its kind before, and its profits must be colossal. Who is at the head of this organization, or even the minor people concerned, I don't know. They've been cleverer than the majority of their kind, for up to now they've made no mistakes.'

'How,' interrupted Mr. Budd, 'do you come into it?'

'Foreign Office Intelligence,' answered Churchman. 'I was loaned to them for this job by MI5.'

Mr. Budd took a long, slow drink. 'I see. I'm not doubtin' your word, but s'pose you've got somethin' ter prove what you say?'

Churchman went over to his desk, took out a bunch of keys, and unlocked a drawer. From it he pulled out a small leather folder the size of a pocket diary. In silence he came back, and held it out to Mr. Budd. It was rather like a passport. There was a photograph of Churchman, a description, a rubber stamp and an official signature. Mr. Budd had seen many similar identification warrants before.

'Good enough,' he said, handing the little folder back. 'We've known at the Yard about this drug gang for some time, of course, but it's outside my department. The Special Branch of the C.I.D. 'ave been 'andlin' it.'

'I know.' Churchman nodded. 'But the Foreign Office was not quite satisfied with the way it was being handled. That's why they gave the job to me.'

'I wish,' remarked Mr. Budd, stifling a yawn, 'that you'd told me this before. It 'ud 'ave saved me a lot o' time an' trouble.'

'My instructions were that I was to work off my own bat,' said Churchman. 'I don't think the F.O. were altogether sure that the police were not in some way involved. I'm disobeying my instructions now by telling you what I am, but I think we shall get better results if we work together from now on. Of course you will treat everything I've said in strict confidence.'

'You can rely on that,' said Mr. Budd. 'Now s'pose you tell me all you've discovered, an' then we'll pool what we know.'

'In some ways it isn't much. For a long time I couldn't get a line at all, and then a chance remark I overheard in a West End bar put me onto The Talking Parrot. I knew quite a lot about Colonel Hautboy, and I thought that I'd probably stumbled on the king pippin. I spent a lot of time at The Talking Parrot, and there's no doubt in my mind that Hautboy is mixed up in the business, but I couldn't find anything definite. It's being run very efficiently and cleverly, I can assure you. The only thing I *did* discover was that quite a number of the regular frequenters of The Talking Parrot sought their entertainment at the

Mammoth Cinema.

'This struck me as peculiar. It's not a West End cinema, and most of the people I'm referring to would have to go a long way to get to it. It occurred to me that possibly I was onto something at last. The thing I couldn't discover was how these drugs were being distributed. It certainly wasn't at The Talking Parrot. But a cinema wouldn't make a bad distributing centre, when you come to think of it. Streams of people of all classes pouring in and out all day and every day. In many respects it was ideal.

'I got a job as foreman by pulling a few strings, and kept my eyes and ears open. But I found out exactly nothing. If the drugs *were* being distributed from the Mammoth Cinema, I couldn't find out how it was being done. The box office was, of course, the obvious possibility. If the cashiers were in the pay of the organization, it would be a simple matter for them to slip small packages of the drugs to the customers with the change and the tickets. They would know to whom, if some sort of password or sign was given when the ticket was issued. But I couldn't see that anything of the kind was happening, and in my capacity of foreman I had a very good opportunity of keeping watch.

'Paula Rivers would have been quite capable of doing it, if she'd been paid well enough, but all her actions were open and above-board so far as I could see. The other cashier, Singer, was equally open in everything she did. In spite of my failure to find out how it was done, however, I was still firmly convinced the cinema *was* being used as the distributing centre. I've seen fashionably dressed women and men arrive looking sick and ill — the trembling wrecks to which drug addicts are reduced when they are deprived of a supply of the drug — and I've seen them leave with firm hands and a firm step, as hale and hearty as anybody else. The obvious conclusion is that somehow, during the time they were in the cinema, a supply of the drug had reached them.'

Mr. Budd nodded. Although he looked in imminent danger of falling asleep, he was listening with keen interest. 'Seems logical,' he murmured. 'What about this gal, Rivers?'

Churchman stubbed out his cigarette and lit another. 'She was killed because she found something out. And, like a little fool, she tried to make money out of it.'

'Blackmail?' said Mr. Budd succinctly.

'Yes; but she was playing with the wrong kind of people.'

'I guessed it was blackmail. She'd been hintin' to her mother that she might be gettin' a lot o' money . . . And what about this whisperin' woman?'

'She puzzles me.' Churchman shook his head and frowned. 'I don't know how she comes into it. She's not one of the organization — at least I don't think so. I thought she might be working for the police . . . ?'

'Nuthin' ter do with us,' said Mr. Budd. 'Whoever she is, she seems ter know a good bit. She knew that gal Rivers was goin' ter be bumped off.'

'Yes.' Churchman inhaled a lungful of smoke and expelled it slowly. His face was worried.

'This feller who come bargin' out of

185

here and knocked into me,' said Mr. Budd. ''E was one of 'em, I suppose?'

'Yes. I'm rather worried about him. It looks as though they were on to me, doesn't it? And *that* means that my usefulness is finished. That's partly the reason why I'm telling you all I know.'

'And what's the rest of the reason?' murmured the stout superintendent.

'So that we can work together. Whatever happens.'

'Well, I'm agreeable to that.'

'I may have to give up my character of Foxlow, though. If they've got onto that, it's going to be more of a liability than an asset. If these people know who I really am, they're not going to do anything to give themselves away.'

'D'you suspect any particular person at the Mammoth Cinema?' asked Mr. Budd.

'No. I could find no reason for suspecting anybody.'

'But if it's bein' used as a distributin' centre for these drugs, one of the staff *must* be responsible.'

Churchman nodded in agreement. 'That's quite right. Unless, of course, it should happen to be a patron. That could be the case, you know.'

Mr. Budd pursed his thick lips, thought for a moment, and slowly shook his head. 'If that *was* the case, there'd be no need to confine themselves to the Mammoth Cinema. Any cinema could be used, couldn't it? No, I should think, if you're right, that it was one of the staff. You 'eard about that feller Figgis, o' course?'

'Yes.'

''E was in it,' said the big man thoughtfully. 'They was afraid 'e would talk, an' so they poisoned 'im. All very neat an' clever.'

'They *are* clever. Damned clever!'

'I don't think there's any doubt that 'Autboy knows all the answers. There was a note we found on Figgis that was signed with a little drawing of a parrot. But it ain't much good *knowin'* if you can't *prove* it.' He yawned widely and long. 'Time I was in bed,' he remarked, getting ponderously to his feet. 'Well, I'm glad that you've been cleared up, if you don't mind me puttin' it that way. An' I'm glad we've 'ad this little talk. I think maybe it'll lead to somethin'.'

'That was the object,' said Churchman, smiling.

'Yes,' said Mr. Budd sleepily. 'Yes, I'm certain that between us we'll be able to put this drug syndicate where it belongs. Good night, sir, an' I don't 'ave ter warn you to take care of yerself.'

'Not after tonight's experience,' affirmed Churchman. He walked with the stout superintendent to the front door of the flat. 'You'd better be careful yourself.'

'I've been careful all me life,' said Mr. Budd, and he went slowly down the stairs.

17

The Woman in the Car

'It's been a lovely evening,' said Eileen, settling back in a corner of the Lagonda with a tired sigh.

'I'll say it has,' agreed George Nicholls enthusiastically. 'Can't remember when I've enjoyed myself so much.'

'We haven't discovered much, though, have we?' said Jimmy Redfern despondently.

His words struck Eileen like a splash of cold water. For the moment she had forgotten the real reason for their visit to The Talking Parrot. 'I suppose we haven't,' she said.

'You can't expect to do everything in one go,' said Nicholls, pressing the starter. 'I don't think we did so badly, really. We know that your sister *did* go quite often to the club.'

'And I'm quite certain that Hautboy

knows more than he said,' put in Jimmy. 'I'm sure he was lying about that box. The sight of it gave him a pretty bad shock, although he tried to hide it.'

'Yes, I noticed that,' said Nicholls, sending the car forward smoothly. 'You know, the person we want to find is this woman — the old woman who gave you that note, Eileen, for your sister, and warned you to get out of the club. She seems to know a lot.'

'The police are trying to find her,' said Jimmy. 'If they can't, is it likely that we can?' He was feeling very tired and suddenly and unaccountably irritable.

'You never know,' said Nicholls. 'But I'll admit it does sound pretty difficult. Like looking for a mythical needle in a problematical haystack, eh? Shall I drop you first, Redfern, and then take Eileen home?'

'Why not the other way round?' said Jimmy, and realized, in astonishment, that the reason for his irritability lay in the attention George Nicholls had been lavishing on Eileen all the evening. Why it should annoy him he didn't trouble to analyse, but it definitely did, the more so because she seemed to like it.

'Just as you like,' said Nicholls. 'When are we having another evening out? What about popping along to The Talking Parrot tomorrow?'

'Oh, I couldn't leave Mother all by herself again so soon,' broke in Eileen. 'I'd love to — I've enjoyed every second of it — but I can't leave her alone too often.'

'What about the next night, then?' persisted Nicholls. 'After all, we've got to follow this thing up, haven't we? I mean, because we didn't find out much tonight, it's no good giving up, is it?'

'Eileen's promised to come out to dinner with me.' What prompted him to make this completely untruthful statement, Jimmy hadn't the least idea. He saw the pale blur that was Eileen's face turn towards him quickly, but he couldn't see the expression of surprise with which she was staring at him.

'Well, make it the following night, then,' said Nicholls doggedly.

'Yes,' Eileen agreed quickly. Her heart

was beating rapidly. Why had Jimmy said that she had promised to go out to dinner with him when he hadn't even asked her? She hardly dared to hope that it was because . . .

'That's fine,' said Nicholls. 'I'll meet you with the car, same time, same place. Will that do?'

Eileen agreed mechanically, her thoughts still full of the wonderful possibility which Jimmy's surprising statement had conjured up. She heard his muttered assent, and turned her head to look out of the window as they pulled up for the traffic lights at a crossing.

A large saloon car slid to a stop beside them and the light of a street lamp fell obliquely through the window, partially illuminating the interior. Idly, her mind still busy with pleasant thoughts, Eileen looked at a person, dimly visible, sitting in the corner. The lights changed as she uttered a sudden exclamation and clutched Jimmy by the arm.

'What's the matter?' he asked quickly.

'The woman in that car,' said Eileen excitedly. 'It was the old woman who stopped me in the street and gave me the note for . . . for Paula.'

'Are you sure?' exclaimed Jimmy.

'Yes, yes. I saw her quite plainly in the light of that lamp!'

He leaned across her and peered out the window. The big saloon had got away quickly when the traffic lights changed and he only caught a glimpse of the red tail-lights.

'We'll follow it,' said Nicholls. 'By Jove, Eileen, if you haven't made a mistake, this is a bit of luck! If we can find out who that woman is and get hold of her, we may find out all we want to know.'

The Lagonda shot forward. The tail-lights of the other car were dwindling in the distance but still plainly visible.

'Don't let them think you're trailing them,' said Jimmy, all his tiredness and irritability gone. 'I should keep a good distance so long as they don't give you the slip.'

'You can trust me,' said George Nicholls joyously. 'They won't get away. I'll back this car against anything on wheels.'

The deserted streets rushed by them smoothly. Lights appeared, flashed, and were gone. The hum of the powerful engine was rhythmic and sure, and they could sense the power that pulsed in the steady vibration. The dark road, lit spasmodically by intermittent lights, receded swiftly behind them, and the red light in front, a vivid speck in the night, went on and on. The street lights grew less and less frequent. Long patches of hedges and trees took the place of the rows of houses and shops.

'Where are we?' asked Jimmy.

Nicholls shook his head, his eyes fixed on the moving points of red that sparkled in the darkness. 'Don't know,' he replied laconically. 'Heading for open country, by the look of it.'

They continued to cover mile after mile, twisting and turning until they lost all sense of direction. There were no lights now; no houses or shops. Only the road before them and the darkness of the night on either side that somehow suggested space.

'How much further are they going?'

muttered Jimmy, lighting a cigarette. 'You're quite sure that you weren't mistaken, Eileen?'

She had been quite sure when she had seen the woman's face in the light of the street standard, but now she was wondering if she might not have been misled by a resemblance. No, she couldn't have been mistaken. It *was* the old woman. There couldn't be two with such an ugly witch-like face.

'It's too late now to worry,' said Nicholls cheerfully. 'I only hope the petrol lasts out.'

They sped through a sleepy village and suddenly the red lights in front disappeared. Nicholls relaxed his foot on the accelerator and the Lagonda slowed. 'Where did it go? Did either of you see?' he asked.

'Must have turned off somewhere,' said Jimmy, leaning forward and peering into the darkness.

'There,' exclaimed Eileen as they passed an open gateway. 'I saw the lights. They turned in through there.'

'Go on and pull up,' said Jimmy. 'We

can come back on foot.'

The road curved a few yards further on and Nicholls stopped the Lagonda round the bend. They got out.

'Look here,' said Nicholls, 'we can't *all* go. You two stay here and I'll have a scout round.'

Jimmy wasn't altogether satisfied with this arrangement, but there was no time to waste in argument, so he agreed. George Nicholls went quickly up the road and disappeared round the bend. The gateway into which the car they had been following had turned proved, on closer inspection, to be the driveway of a large house. He could dimly see the bulk of the house itself among some trees; and as he slipped cautiously in at the open gate, a light came on in one of the ground floor windows. The curtains had not been drawn, and the light poured out across the drive and illuminated the car, which was standing in front of a pillared porch.

Nicholls crept carefully up the broad drive, treading with care so that his footsteps should make no sound on the gravel. Presently he reached the shelter of a clump of bushes that grew almost exactly opposite the lighted window, and found that by craning his neck that he could see into the room. It was well-furnished in a bygone period, and the portion he could see was empty. Then a man came into view — a middle-aged man with a completely bald head. He was smoking a cigar and seemed to be talking to someone who was invisible to the watching Nicholls. He kept vanishing and reappearing as he paced up and down. Nicholls decided that he would like to see a great deal more of that room. He was particularly anxious to see who the bald man was talking to.

He left the shelter of the bushes, tiptoed across the drive and picked his way through a bed of bush roses that grew immediately beneath the window. And now, as he crouched with his eyes just above the sill, he could see the whole room.

An old woman dressed in shabby black was sitting in a chair by a small table. She was holding a cigarette in a claw-like hand, and her nutcracker jaws were moving rapidly as she spoke to the bald man, who had stopped his perambulations and was standing looking down at her. Nicholls thought he had seldom seen a more repulsive-looking woman. She was just like the illustration of a witch in a child's fairytale book. He strained his ears to try and hear what she was saying but couldn't.

The bald man made a sudden impatient gesture with the cigar and once more began to pace up and down. He was frowning now and looked ill-tempered. Suddenly he swung round and began to speak rapidly and apparently urgently. The old woman listened, nodding every now and again.

And then, without warning, a hand suddenly gripped Nicholls by the collar, and he was jerked to his feet.

'Spyin', eh?' growled a man's voice. 'Caught yer pretty neat, ain't I? You just come along an' explain who yer are and wot you're a-doin' here.'

18

Gone!

Eileen threw the cigarette she had been smoking out of the window and turned to Jimmy. 'George has been gone a long time,' she said with a trace of anxiety. 'Do you think he's all right?'

'I don't see what can have happened to him,' Jimmy replied. 'He's probably snooping round to see what he can find out.'

'Supposing he's been caught?'

'H'm! I should hardly think it's likely, but perhaps I'd better go along and see.'

'I'll come with you.'

'You won't do anything of the sort,' Jimmy said, opening the door of the car.

'I'd much rather come with you.'

'Stay here where it's safer,' he retorted briefly, and got out.

'Jimmy, do be careful,' she whispered after him as he faded away in the darkness.

Although he had said little to Eileen, Jimmy was feeling very uneasy as he walked rapidly up the road. George had been gone for the greater part of an hour. Surely something must have happened to have kept him all that time. He came to the driveway and paused, peering up the dark drive. Darkness met his eyes. Darkness everywhere.

He entered the gateway and groped his way up the drive. Presently he came to the house, a great mass of blackness that was only just visible. This was where the car had come, but there was no sign of it now. The gravelled space before the portico was empty.

Jimmy stood looking about him, wondering what to do next. The house was completely dark and quite silent. It looked as if the inmates were all asleep. And what had become of George Nicholls?

After a few moments' hesitation, Jimmy decided to explore further. As noiselessly as he could, he moved forward. The gravelled drive led round the corner of the house and ended at a garage, the doors of which were shut. The car, then, had been put away, he thought. Beside the garage was an arched opening that evidently led to the back of the premises. Jimmy stepped through it and found himself in a paved passage that ended in a wide loggia, beyond which was the garden. Everything here was as dark and silent as the front. He walked the entire length of the house and back again. Nothing. No sign of life in the place and no sign of George Nicholls. What could have become of him?

Jimmy stood in the shadow of the loggia, uncertain what to do next. It seemed pretty useless staying where he was. The most sensible thing he could do was to go back to Eileen. Perhaps George had gone back another way and he had missed him.

Worried, puzzled and uneasy, he made his way back to the gate and walked swiftly up the road. But as he rounded the bend, a shock awaited him. The car and Eileen had gone. There was the clump of trees and the gate in the hedgerow where George had parked it, but of the car and

Eileen there was no sign at all.

Jimmy walked quickly forward and then stood staring up and down the deserted road. What could have happened during the short time he had been away? Eileen wasn't likely to have driven off. She wouldn't do that, leaving them both behind — even if she could drive a car, which he doubted. Puzzled, confused and worried, he pulled out a cigarette and lit it. What ought he to do? Beyond the fact that he was somewhere out in the country, he had no idea where he was.

He went over and sat on the gate, puffing at his cigarette and trying to think things out. Not only George Nicholls, but now Eileen and the car had disappeared. Obviously there was a connection between the disappearance and the old woman in the car; that was pretty certain. They had got George, and while Jimmy had been snooping round the house looking for him they had got Eileen. They must be somewhere inside that house. How the old woman and the people working with her had managed it in the case of Eileen and the car, he couldn't imagine, but they evidently had. It was up to him to do something — but what?

The sensible thing, perhaps, would be to go to the police, but he had no idea where the nearest station was to be found. In the meanwhile, anything might happen to Eileen and George. Perhaps he ought to go back to the house and see if he could find any trace of them. He flung away his cigarette and got down off the gate. As he walked back along the dark and silent road, he tried to work out a plan.

What did one do in an emergency like this? What *could* one do? He had seen situations like this in the films; had read of similar ones in books; but it didn't help him very much. This was *real*.

He reached the open gateway once more without being able to evolve any reasonable plan of campaign. All he could do, he thought, was to trust to luck. Maybe something would give him an idea. He went up the drive past the garage and round to the back of the house. It was still in complete darkness.

He stood looking at it, frowning and biting his lip. If only he could get inside. Well, maybe he could; perhaps there was a window left unlatched. It was worth trying, anyhow. Anything was better than just standing about doing nothing.

He inspected the long windows opening onto the loggia, but they were all tightly shut and fastened and were, moreover, protected by shutters on the inside. He went round what he thought was probably the kitchen region. There were several windows here, and presently he found a small one that was partly open. It looked as though it might belong to a pantry or larder. It was held in the half-open position by an iron bar that was secured by a stud in the frame. Reaching up, Jimmy very carefully lifted the bar off the stud and pulled the window fully open. It didn't look very large. With a fervent hope that he wouldn't get stuck halfway, he pulled himself up and wriggled his way in. It was a very tight squeeze indeed, and he only just succeeded.

It was quite dark within, and when he

was half across the sill he got out his lighter with difficulty and snapped it on to see where he was. As he had expected, it was a small larder. The walls were lined with shelves, and these were laden with tins, jars and articles of food. Just below the window, through which he was balanced precariously, was a wide shelf stacked with tinned food, and he was thankful that he had taken the precaution of using the lighter. If he had continued to wriggle his way through the window without looking to see where he was going, he would have brought the whole lot down, and the clatter would have been appalling.

Even as it was, he had great difficulty getting from the window to the safety of the floor without disturbing the contents of the shelf. He managed it at last and tried the door. It was not locked, and he breathed a sigh of relief. It opened into a large kitchen that was partially illuminated by a dim light coming through a partially open door.

Jimmy Redfern, with his heart thumping wildly, tiptoed across to this door and looked out. He spied a passage, at the end of which was the main hall. The light came from a shaded bulb in the ceiling, and he could hear the faint murmur of voices.

Hardly daring to breathe, he picked his way along the passage. The murmur grew louder, and he discovered that it came from behind a closed door to the right of the hall. Reaching it, he stooped down and looked through the keyhole. He could see nothing. The key was in the lock on the inside and obstructing his vision. He was wondering what he should do next when the door was suddenly opened and, losing his balance, he almost fell into the room beyond.

★   ★   ★

Mr. Budd was a very tired man when he arrived at the Yard on the morning following his interview with Mr. Church-man. He had had about three hours' sleep altogether, and he liked a lot of sleep. The first thing he did when he reached his cheerless little office was to get on the house phone to the officer-in-charge of the dangerous drugs branch. They had quite a long conversation, which resulted in the arrival of a messenger with a bulky folder which Mr. Budd signed for and proceeded to peruse with great care and the assistance of one of his thin black cigars. He spent the greater part of the morning over this, and when he had finished and sent the folder back he leaned back in his chair and cocked a thoughtful eye at the ceiling.

Churchman had not exaggerated. The peddling of dope had increased to alarming proportions during the preceding eighteen months. Several arrests had apparently been made, but they were all small fry. Questioning them had elicited nothing — not because they wouldn't talk, but because they knew nothing.

The syndicate *were* clever, thought the big man. They hadn't so much covered their tracks — they had made no tracks to cover. Whoever was at the head of affairs was a genius at organization. Colonel Hautboy? Mr. Budd shook his head. He knew quite a lot about the colonel, but he didn't think that he filled the bill. It was someone with a different type of mentality. The big man had an idea that it was someone new to crime and therefore all the more difficult to catch. It was the amateurs who usually got away with it — for a time at any rate, until they went on too long. The methods of the police were nearly perfect so far as catching the professional crook was concerned; but the amateur, if he was clever, could beat them every time. The *modus operandi* method was useless with him. There was no precedent to go on, unless he went on too long and stamped his work with the personal characteristics that made it easily recognizable. Which, luckily, he usually did.

Just before lunch, a call came through from Inspector Longfoot that sent Mr. Budd hurrying along to see him. He found a greatly worried man in the inspector's room at the local police station.

'They've gone — all three of 'em,' said Longfoot. 'Mrs. Rivers, Eileen Rivers and Redfern. One of my men was tailing

Redfern last night when he called for the woman. They both left, togged up in evening clothes, and were picked up by a feller in a Lagonda. That was where my man lost 'em.'

'What about Mrs. Rivers?' asked Mr. Budd.

'A big closed car called for her early this morning,' answered the worried Longfoot. 'One of the neighbours saw her get into it and it drove away.'

''Ow did you find all this out?'

'I was checking up on Redfern. He hadn't been home all night and he hadn't turned up at the place he works. We went round to Eden Street to see if they knew anything about him. We couldn't make anyone hear when we knocked, and then the woman next door told us about the car.'

'Hm!' The big man fingered his fleshy chin and frowned. 'It's queer — very queer . . . '

'It looks to me as though Redfern has made a bolt for it,' declared the inspector.

'What about this feller — the chap in the Lagonda?'

'He's a feller called George Nicholls, a customer at the garage where Redfern works. He ain't been home neither.'

'It's hardly likely that all of 'em 'ud made a bolt for it,' remarked Mr. Budd thoughtfully. 'I don't understand it.'

'I'm going to get hauled over the coals for this,' grunted the inspector, 'unless Redfern can be found.'

'Have you had his description circulated?'

'I've had *all* their descriptions circulated.'

'Who's this feller — what's-'is-name — Nicholls?' murmured the stout superintendent. 'D'yer know anything about 'im?'

Longfoot shook his head. 'No,' he answered. 'Except that he's well off — I suppose you'd call him rich.'

''Ow does 'e get his money?' asked Mr. Budd quickly.

'Private income, I suppose. He don't do any work.'

'Oh, 'e doesn't, eh?' remarked Mr. Budd, almost completely closing his eyes and pinching his nose delicately between finger and thumb. 'Doesn't do any work, eh? Maybe it 'ud be worth inquiring a bit more into 'im.' He fished a cigar out of his waistcoat pocket and thoughtfully bit off the end. 'I believe I've found out what's at the back o' this business,' he added.

'You have?' Longfoot became suddenly interested.

Mr. Budd nodded slowly. 'Wait till I get this thing alight an' I'll tell yer.'

Longfoot watched the deliberate operation apprehensively. He had suffered from Mr. Budd's cigars before. When he had puffed out several evil-smelling clouds of smoke with immense satisfaction, the stout superintendent proceeded to tell him about the dope ring. He was careful to keep his promise to Churchman, and he carefully omitted any mention of that gentleman's name. The inspector listened with the greatest attention.

'Well, this puts a different complexion on it,' he commented when Mr. Budd had finished. 'It looks to me like a big thing.'

'A *very* big thing,' agreed the detective.

'You think this chap Nicholls may be the king pippin?'

'I won't go so far as to say that,' said Mr. Budd cautiously. 'But he's well worth investigatin'. I'd like ter know where this money of his comes from. Of course it may be all open an' innocent, an' then again it may not. If it is, it shouldn't be difficult to find out the source. Now that's a nice little job for Leek — if 'e can keep awake long enough.'

He left Longfoot soon after and went back to the Yard. The disappearance of Mrs. Rivers, Redfern, Eileen and Nicholls puzzled him. It was unexpected and unaccountable. Why had they gone, and where had they gone to?

He thought that Churchman ought to know about this latest development, and decided to go over to the Mammoth Cinema after he had seen Leek. The melancholy sergeant came in ten minutes late.

'Oh, 'ere you are,' grunted Mr. Budd. 'One day you'll be early an' everyone'll think the clocks are wrong.'

'I 'ad ter wait a long time for a bus,' explained Leek.

'It's wonderful 'ow these buses seem ter dodge you. I can't say I blame 'em. If I was a bus an' I saw you waitin', I'd take another route. Now look here — I've got a job fer you.' He explained, and Leek listened with a gloomy expression.

'When do I start?' asked the sergeant without enthusiasm.

'Now,' answered Mr. Budd, reaching for his hat. 'I'm goin' along to the Mammoth Cinema and I shan't be comin' back 'ere ternight. Report in the mornin', and don't be more'n a couple of hours late.'

'Mr. Foxlow' was on duty in the vestibule when he arrived. 'I'd like to have a word with you in private,' said Mr. Budd.

'I'll be going for my tea in five minutes,' whispered Churchman. 'Cafe ten yards along on this side. Shillin', one-an'-six on the right — two-an'-three an' two-an'-nine h'on the left.'

The big man drifted away. He found the little eating house and sat down at one of the stained tables. A tired-looking woman brought him a mug of very strong tea and a wedge of indigestible cake, which she slapped down with such force that the tea slopped over and the cake almost shot off the plate.

There were only three people in the place, and Mr. Budd sipped his tea and munched his cake while he awaited the arrival of Mr. Churchman. It was about ten minutes before he came in and sat down opposite the big man.

'The tea is terrible and the cake's worse,' he remarked in a low voice. 'Sorry I had to suggest this place, but . . . '

'I've been in worse,' said Mr. Budd, pushing aside his empty plate.

'What did you want to see me about?'

'There's bin a development which I thought — ' began Mr. Budd, but he stopped as the tired-looking woman lounged up.

''Ullo, 'andsome,' she greeted. 'Wotcher want?'

'H'if I told yer, Em'ly, you'd smack me face,' answered Churchman, reverting to the nasal accent of Foxlow.

'Get on with yer,' said the woman. 'Tea, is it?' 'An' a slice o' cake,' said Churchman. 'Bin in this week yet?'

'Comin' ternight,' said the woman.

'With 'Arry, I s'pose?'

'Wot's it got ter do with you 'oo I'm goin' with?' she demanded.

'H'if yer was comin' alone, I might slip in fer a bit an' 'old yer 'and.'

'You've got an 'ope,' she retorted scornfully. 'Think you're James Mason, don't yer?'

'Bet I wouldn't 'ave ter wait fer me tea if I was. Get a move on, sweet'eart. I've on'y got a quarter of an hour.'

The woman shrugged her thin shoulders and sauntered away.

'You were saying?' Churchman leaned across to Mr. Budd.

The big man told him briefly.

'It looks serious to me. What about this man Nicholls?'

'It's queer you should say that,' remarked Mr. Budd. 'The same idea struck me.'

'He *could* be the man we're looking for,' said Churchman thoughtfully.

215

'An' again he may not. But I'm havin' 'im inquired into all the same.'

'I think you're very wise,' agreed Churchman. 'Thank yer, sweet'eart. I 'ope yer've put plenty o' sugar in it?'

'You've got yer ration, an' not so much of the 'sweetheart',' snapped the waitress, banging a mug of tea and a plate of cake in front of him. 'I'm partic'lar who I allows to get familiar with me, see.'

'That's wot I like about yer,' said Churchman. 'No makin' yerself cheap like some on 'em.'

She tossed her head and walked away.

'I think you're wise,' he repeated when she had gone. 'You may not find it so easy, though, to discover anything suspicious if he *is* the man we think he might be.'

Mr. Budd went home to his little house at Streatham with a lot to occupy his mind. He had an additional problem to puzzle over the following morning, for he had only been in his office three minutes when Inspector Longfoot rang up to say that Jimmy Redfern, Eileen, Mrs. Rivers and George Nicholls had all returned and refused to offer any explanation for their absence.

19

Mr. Budd Seeks Inspiration

Mr. Budd questioned them himself later on that day, but he achieved no better result than Longfoot. Redfern and Nicholls practically told him in so many words to mind his own business. If they chose to stay out all night, they said, they were at perfect liberty to do so; and they were not compelled to say why, or where they had been. Eileen and her mother were more polite about it but equally uncommunicative.

Mr. Budd, irritable and weary, gave it up. 'They don't intend to talk and that's that,' he said to Longfoot. 'An' we can't make 'em.'

'It's very queer,' began the inspector.

'There may be nuthin' in it. Maybe they *did* spend the night with some friends, or goin' fer a drive.'

'Do you think so?' asked Longfoot.

'No, I don't,' snapped the big man, 'but what can we do about it? Nuthin'. We 'aven't the least idea what 'appened to 'em.'

'If it was all innocent and above-board, why don't they tell us?' said Longfoot reasonably. 'It's darned fishy, if you ask me.'

Mr. Budd thought so too. He searched his brain for an explanation but he couldn't find one. It was scarcely likely that Eileen and her mother could be mixed up in the drug traffic and Paula's murder — unless, of course, they had discovered something and were being frightened into keeping silent. That might be it. Knowing what had happened to Paula, it wouldn't be difficult to scare them. But surely not so easy to scare Nicholls? Then again, perhaps Nicholls was not the one to be scared, but the scarer? If they had somehow or other discovered that he was the man responsible for it all, he might have silenced them with threats of the consequences if they spoke. It wasn't a very satisfactory explanation, thought Mr. Budd, but it was the best he could find. *Something* had happened to all four of them during that mysterious absence, and it seemed too much of a coincidence to suppose that it had no connection with the death of Paula Rivers and the drug organization.

It was all very perplexing, and Mr. Budd wasn't at all happy about it. Although he had learned what was behind the murder of Paula Rivers, he was no nearer to discovering who had shot her than he had been when he started. Or who had poisoned Ted Figgis.

If only he could get a line to the whispering woman, that mysterious individual who had cropped up so often and who seemed to know so much. How exactly did she fit into the business? She wasn't, apparently, working with the drug syndicate, because she had tried to warn Paula of her danger. But if she was working against these people, what was her motive? And why didn't she come openly to the police and tell them what she knew?

Mr. Budd thought he would give a lot

for a little talk with her, but she had completely vanished. Every policeman in the country was on the lookout for her, but they had been unsuccessful. He was a little disgruntled when Sergeant Leek came into the office that afternoon to make his report.

'There don't seem ter be anythin' suspicious about this feller Nicholls,' said Leek wearily. 'Is father was in the woollen trade an' 'e left 'im a fortune, which Nicholls seems ter be spendin' as fast as 'e can. 'E's what they call a playboy.'

'Racin', cards, nightclubs, an' women, eh?' remarked Mr. Budd.

'That's right. Seems to 'ave got the reputation of bein' a good ol' feller.'

'Thought you said there was nuthin' suspicious about 'im,' grunted his superior. 'I'm always suspicious of a man who's got the reputation fer bein' a good ol' feller.'

'Well, you know what I mean,' said Leek.

Mr. Budd nodded. 'I've got another job for you,' he said. 'I want to know all about Lord Penstemmon.'

'I'll get goin' on it first thin' in the mornin'.'

'You'll get goin' on it *now,*' snapped Mr. Budd.

The sergeant's long face fell. 'I was plannin' a nice quiet evenin',' he said dolefully. 'I've bin trampin' about seein' people an' askin' questions until me feet aches an' me throat's dry.'

'That's what you get paid for. What else d'yer want, money fer jam?'

'I don't like jam. Give me a pot o' real good marmalade an' you can 'ave all yer jam.'

'I was speakin' figuratively. I don't care whether yer like jam, honey, treacle, fish-paste, or what-'ave-you. I've no interest in your gluttonous desires.'

'I'm a very small eater,' said Leek defensively. 'Nobody could call me a glutton.'

'I could call you lots o' things,' said the exasperated Mr. Budd, 'an' you'll hear every one of 'em if you don't get started on that job right away. Now get goin'.'

The melancholy sergeant departed with a long sigh, grumbling under his breath.

Mr. Budd put his feet up on the desk, fished a cigar out of his waistcoat pocket, frowned at it for a moment, bit off the end, stuck it in his mouth and lit it. Surrounded by clouds of smoke, he sat with his eyes half-closed and thought. It was one of his practices, when his thoughts were what he called 'in a muddle', to allow his brain to relax completely and let them sort themselves out. He made no attempt to marshal them in any order, but let them come as they would. First one and then another would thrust its way to the fore, a jumbled mixture, but gradually they would begin to drop into place like the pieces of a puzzle, and form a kind of pattern.

Sometimes this pattern was dim and difficult to discern, but he had learned from experience that if the process was continued, and no attempt was made to force it, it gradually became clearer until the pattern stood out clear and bright. It might not be a method for everyone, but in Mr. Budd's case it worked — sometimes. He tried it now.

The cigar burned slowly away, and he lit another. Something was trying to push its way up out of the chaotic confusion in his mind. He sat on, motionless, his eyes closed and cigar ash snowing down over his capacious waistcoat.

*   *   *

Colonel Hautboy was also smoking a cigar — a fragrant blend of Havana leaf that was very different to the rank, evil-smelling cheroots that Mr. Budd was so fond of. He sat in a deep chair in his comfortable flat above The Talking Parrot; and to judge from the expression on his face, his thoughts were far from pleasant. At his elbow stood a half-empty bottle of Johnny Walker and a partially filled glass.

Colonel Hautboy was uneasy. Several things had combined to produce his uneasiness, but the most potent of these was the delivery of the marcasite box. That had shaken him to the core. He thought that it was time to get out of this drugs racket that had proved so profitable. The trouble was, he didn't quite know how to do it. The man who had been responsible for getting him into it disliked quitters and had a most unpleasant way of dealing with them. At the first hint that he wanted to break away there would be trouble, and Colonel Hautboy had spent his life trying to avoid all forms of trouble.

But the red light was blazing steadily. The killing of Paula Rivers had been a mistake. It was likely, he thought, to prove a fatal one for those involved. It had turned a floodlight of publicity on their operations, which before had been con-ducted safely and profitably in the dark. Paula Rivers should have been paid to keep her mouth shut. They could have easily afforded to do so, and she would never have given them away so long as the money was coming in.

Yes, killing her had been a bad move. There were other methods that would have had the same effect. She was the type who could, without much difficulty, have been persuaded to become an addict herself, and an overdose would have done the trick. Her murder had been bungled, and as a result they were all in jeopardy.

Hautboy picked up his glass and drank the remainder of the whisky. He wished that he had never become mixed up in this business. It was true that he had made a lot of money, but money wasn't much use in a prison cell, and he had an unpleasant conviction that that was where they were all heading. All of them, of course, except the man at the top.

Nobody knew him. He conducted all the business, issued all his instructions, over the telephone. He could slip out without anyone being the wiser, leaving the rest to carry the baby. A nice set-up, thought Hautboy.

He finished his cigar, went into his bathroom, and turned on the hot tap. He shaved, took a bath, and dressed carefully. He was pouring himself out another drink when the telephone rang. For a moment or two he looked at the instrument with the bottle of Johnny Walker poised over the glass. Then with a jerk of his shoulders he put it down, walked over and picked up the receiver.

The voice that came over the wire left no doubt as to the identity of the caller. Colonel Hautboy listened while the voice spoke rapidly and with its habitual tonelessness. And as he listened, his face went white.

'You're mad,' he whispered.

'I'm immensely sane,' retorted the voice, 'and I don't require your criticism. You will do as you're told.'

'But it's sheer madness,' protested Hautboy. 'Why not let us get out while the going's good?'

'I shall expect my instructions to be carried out,' said the voice coldly, and there was a click as the caller rang off.

Colonel Hautboy took out his handkerchief and wiped his moist face, then poured himself out half a tumbler of neat whisky, which he swallowed at a gulp. His smooth white hands were shaking, and his face was grey, for the man on the telephone had ordered murder.

20

Into the Night

Mr. Budd left Scotland Yard just before six, a tired and irritable man. His method, which usually produced results, had completely failed him. The nebulous something that had tried to force its way to the fore had receded without taking tangible form. It was still there, buried somewhere under the mass of other odds and ends in his brain, and the only hope was that it might suddenly manifest itself. It was useless trying to make it. That nearly always had the reverse effect. The only thing to be done was to forget all about it and let his subconscious work away on its own.

He got into his shabby little car and drove home to his neat little villa in Streatham. He would have a good meal and a bottle of beer, do a couple of hours' gardening, and go to bed early. The murder of Paula Rivers and the drug syndicate would be put out of his mind completely; he would come back to both fresh in the morning.

He put his car away and let himself in with his key. His dour housekeeper, of whom he went in secret dread, met him in the hall.

'You're home early,' she said in a voice that sounded entirely disapproving.

Mr. Budd agreed. He would have agreed as readily whatever she had said. He made it a habit never to disagree with her.

'I'll get you a meal,' she announced in the manner of a queen conferring a favour upon a humble subject. 'It'll be ready by the time you've washed.'

Mr. Budd departed with the meekness of a schoolboy to the spotless bathroom.

The meal *was* ready when he came down to the little dining-room, and it was a very tasty and substantial one. When he had eaten and finished the bottle of beer, he lit a cigar and went out into the garden. Roses were a passion with Mr. Budd, and his little garden was full of them. It was some while since he had been able to spare any time for them, and he looked forward to spending the remainder of the evening hoeing and weeding and spraying, refreshed by the smell of the soil.

He forgot his profession and concentrated on his hobby. Although the garden was spick and span, he found plenty to do and worked happily until it was too dark to see. Then he went regretfully indoors, drank another bottle of beer, and had a hot bath.

At ten o'clock he went to bed and read a new book on rose-growing for an hour. A church clock was chiming half-past eleven when he fell asleep.

The same clock was striking two when a closed car came slowly down the road in which Mr. Budd lived. It moved with scarcely a sound, the powerful engine pulsing almost silently. It glided past Mr. Budd's house and drew up at the kerb in the darkest portion of the street. Two men got out of it and walked back quickly to the big man's house. They moved without noise, their feet encased in rubber-soled shoes. Without troubling to open the gate, they vaulted the low wall, heedless of the damage they did to Mr. Budd's beloved bush roses.

They made their way round to the back of the house and stopped outside the kitchen window. The taller of the two took something out of his pocket, and there was the faintest scraping noise. The other dabbed something on the glass of the window; and when, after a second or two, he pulled it away, a small circle of glass came with it. The tall man put a gloved hand through the hole and fumbled for the catch. Inch by inch the window was raised, and both men climbed inside.

Mr. Budd slept soundly. He lay on his back with his mouth half-open and uttered a series of strange grunts and snorts. There was a slight sound at the door, but the sleeping man heard nothing and continued to snore jerkily. The door began to open slowly, and a man's head covered by a handkerchief tied round nose and chin was thrust cautiously through the aperture. Mr. Budd uttered a groaning gasp and turned over on his side. The man at the door stiffened, but the sleeper did not wake. The door opened wider, and the intruder came into the room. For a moment he stood just inside the doorway, his companion looming up behind him. His hand was thrust into the front of his jacket and now he drew it out, holding the squat shape of an automatic. He took a quick step forward toward the bed.

Something struck him across the ankles and he pitched forward, falling with a crash that shook the house. His companion uttered a smothered oath and, turning, fled down the stairs.

Mr. Budd woke, sat up in bed, and switched on the light.

The man who had fallen over the thin trip-wire stretched before the door from hooks in the skirting-board a foot from the floor, which the stout superintendent always took the precaution of fixing before he went to sleep, was scrambling to his feet and groping for the pistol which had been jerked out of his hand. Mr. Budd flung himself out of bed and onto the man before he could recover it. His enormous weight knocked the breath out of the helpless intruder.

Mr. Budd sat on his stomach and pinioned his arms by the wrists. 'Payin' me a call, eh?' he panted. 'Well, well . . . Wasn't prepared for my little booby-trap, was yer?'

The man grunted and tried to struggle free, but the big man held him firmly. 'You can't go as easy as that,' he said. 'I want ter know more about you — a lot more.' He reached suddenly for the gun and, with surprising agility for so stout a man, got to his feet. 'Get up,' he ordered sharply. 'Get up, an' take that thing off your face.'

The man uttered a string of curses.

'Cut that out,' snapped Mr. Budd, 'an' get up.' He prodded him with his foot. The man pulled himself up by the foot of the bed and stood, breathing jerkily. 'Now, let's see what you look like,' said Mr. Budd. He stepped forward and pulled the handkerchief down. The scowling face that stared at him was strange to him. 'Hm! You're a new one on me. Who sent you?'

The intruder remained silent.

'Not going to talk, eh? Well, perhaps yer'll change your mind when you've been in a cell for a bit.'

'What's all the noise about?' Mr. Budd's housekeeper, draped in a quilted dressing-gown, appeared in the doorway. Her voice was disapproving; her expression was disapproving; she radiated disapproval. 'Who is this man?'

'I don't know,' said Mr. Budd, 'and I'd *like* to know.'

'What is he doing here at this time of night?'

'What *are* you doing here?' demanded Mr. Budd, but the captive only glared at him sullenly and made no reply. 'He won't talk,' said the big man, shaking his head. 'Will you go down an' telephone the perlice station? Ask 'em to send a couple o' men round at once.'

The housekeeper stalked away.

'Now we'll soon 'ave you fixed up nice an' comfy,' said Mr. Budd. 'And I'd advise you to find yer tongue.'

'You go to hell,' said the man.

'You're a very foolish feller,' murmured Mr. Budd, sitting down on the side of the bed but keeping a wary eye on the prisoner. 'You'd be wise if you come clean an' told me all you know.'

The housekeeper came back. 'They're sending some men up immediately,' she said calmly. 'I shall now go back to bed, and I should be obliged if you would be as quiet as possible. I do not like being disturbed.' She departed with great dignity.

Mr. Budd shook his head sadly. 'I'm afraid you've annoyed 'er,' he said, 'an' I'm sorry about that, because when she's annoyed it takes 'er about a week ter get over it. Keep still! I ain't used ter firearms, an' this thin' might go off in me excitement.'

The man, who had made a slight movement, stiffened.

Mr. Budd sat and watched him in silence for several minutes, and then there was a loud knock on the door below. 'Come on,' said the stout superintendent, getting up. 'You go first, an' don't forget I've still got this gun.'

He shepherded the man out of the bedroom and down the stairs to the front door. Two men, a sergeant and a constable, came in when he opened the door.

''Ere you are,' said Mr. Budd cheerfully, nodding at his prisoner. 'Take 'im along an' lock 'im up in the cooler. I'll come along an' charge 'im as soon as I'm dressed. Take good care of 'im. I believe he's got some important information to give us.'

'You've got a hope,' grunted the man.

'I'm full of 'ope. Now get along. I'll be down at the station in about ten minutes.' The prisoner was marched off between the constable and the sergeant, and the big man shut the front door and went upstairs to dress.

The police station was not very far away — barely five minutes from Mr. Budd's neat little house. The prisoner went quietly enough, walking in silence between his escorts.

The sergeant was the first to notice the car that came swiftly down the street, but he paid little attention to it because cars

were not uncommon in that neighbour-
hood even so late at night. It was only
when it slowed and drew into the kerb
that he really gave it more than a passing
thought — and then it was too late.

A pencil of orange flame shot from the
back window, and the sergeant went
down with a bullet in his chest, writhing
on the pavement. The prisoner jerked
himself free from the astonished and
alarmed constable, jumped into the car
— which accelerated instantly, and was
halfway down the street before he had
closed the door.

21

Mr. Foxlow Resigns

Mr. Budd heard the whole story from the dejected constable when he arrived at the police station ten minutes later to charge the prisoner who wasn't there.

'It all 'appened in a flash, as you might say,' said the policeman. He was very young, and not a little scared of the wrath that he expected to descend upon him. 'This 'ere car came up alongside us, an' then there was a shot, an' the sergeant was kickin' about on the pavement!'

'I ought to 'ave expected somethin' of the sort,' grunted Mr. Budd. 'Don't you worry yerself, young feller. You couldn't 'elp it. How's the sergeant?'

'Not very badly hurt, sir,' put in the inspector in charge. 'The bullet smashed a rib and was deflected, luckily. He'll be all right again in a few days. Who was this man who got away?'

'I'd like to be able to answer that,' said Mr. Budd grimly. 'An' even more, I'd like ter know who sent 'im. I'm not very popular with somebody, which means they think I know more'n what I do.'

The inspector was a little mystified, but he tactfully refrained from asking questions, and Mr. Budd went back home. He made himself some tea, and, ensconced in a big armchair in his small drawing-room, thought and smoked until it was light. Then he went out and made a search for the means by which the intruder had got in. The job had been accomplished with a professional neatness that roused his admiration, and he discovered by the footprints in the flowerbed in the front garden that two men had been involved. One had evidently got away and waited to rescue his confederate. All very methodical, thought the big man. He was annoyed at the damage they had done to his roses and spent a considerable time doing what he could to repair it. When he had finished he went into the house, shaved, had a wash and came downstairs again to find his housekeeper up and the breakfast ready. She made, to his relief, no reference at all to the night's disturbance.

While Mr. Budd ate a thoughtful meal at Streatham, Colonel Hautboy conducted an unpleasant interview in the bedroom of his flat above The Talking Parrot.

'The whole thing has been bungled,' he declared angrily, pacing up and down in a flowery dressing-gown. 'There were two of you. Surely you could've made a better job of it! Why did you run away when Kahn fell over that confounded wire? If you'd stayed, you could've settled the business then and there.'

'It's all very well to talk,' growled the man who had accompanied Kahn to Mr. Budd's house during the night. 'You wasn't there. I did what I thought was best. How was I to know what had happened? All I heard was a tremendous din. I thought Kahn had been copped, and I cleared off so that I could have a chance of rescuing him later.'

'It was a gross piece of mismanagement!' snapped Hautboy. 'You had a chance you'll never get again, because now this detective fellow will be on his guard, and you muffed it. All the excuses in the world can't alter *that*. And then you had to go and shoot a police sergeant, just to make matters worse.'

'I don't see that that matters — ' began Kahn, but he stopped as Hautboy swung round and faced him.

'Oh you don't, eh?' he said unpleasantly. 'You don't know a lot about the English police, do you? Let me tell you this. If you kill or injure one of them, the rest will never let up until they get you.'

'Oh, shucks!' broke in Kahn. 'How are they goin' to know it was me?'

'I'm hoping they're not. But this man Budd is no fool, for all that he looks like a cow with sleeping sickness. He's one of the cleverest men in the C.I.D., and he's going to start wondering just why an attack should have been made on him.'

'Well, wondering won't get him very far,' muttered the other man. 'Me and Kahn didn't leave any traces. I'll take a big bet on that.'

'It's not you and Kahn he's going to start wondering about. It's who sent you.

That's what he's going to wonder about.'

'Well, I don't see how he can get on to you.'

'He knows that the Rivers woman came to this club, doesn't he?' snarled the colonel. 'He knows that, and he already thinks I know more about her than I've admitted.'

'So what? He can't prove anything.'

'You'd better make yourself scarce,' said Colonel Hautboy abruptly. 'Go down to Frank's place — both of you — and stop there until you hear from me.' He pulled a wad of notes from the pocket of his dressing-gown, skinned half a dozen, and thrust them into Kahn's hand. 'I'll send you some more money if you need it, but don't come anywhere near here. You understand?'

'Got the wind up yer pretty badly, haven't you?' sneered Kahn, pocketing the notes.

'I believe in taking precautions. Budd's seen you and he'll remember you. There'll be a description of you circulated to every policeman in the country within the next few hours, with instructions to pull you in on sight. You'd better shave off that moustache and brush your hair a different way. Now get going, and stop at Frank's until I tell you it's safe to leave.'

He escorted them to the lift, and when they had gone, came back and poured himself out a stiff whisky, which he gulped down neat. Hautboy was verging on something very near to panic. He had been against this Budd business from the start. In his opinion, it was stupid and unnecessary. There had been no danger from Budd. He hadn't got on to anything important, so why go to all this trouble to put him out of the way?

And it hadn't worked. Hautboy had never believed that it *would* work, but he had to obey orders. And now he was left holding the baby. If there was any trouble coming from it, it would be he who would get it. The man who had issued the orders was safely entrenched behind a mask of anonymity.

Colonel Hautboy poured himself out another drink from the Johnny Walker bottle, and cursed the day he had been dragged into the whole business. He'd had no choice in the matter from the moment when he had first heard the unknown's voice over the telephone. How he had become possessed of his knowledge concerning that episode in Hautboy's life, which could still have sent him down for a ten-year stretch, the colonel had no idea. He thought nobody except himself and a man who was dead knew about that. But the voice on the telephone had quickly undeceived him, and from then on he had been forced to do what the other had demanded.

He finished his second drink, lighted a cigarette, and sat down in an easy chair. It would be as well to be prepared for a quick getaway, he thought. At any moment something might happen to explode the mine that he had sensed ticking away under his feet ever since the shooting of Paula Rivers.

He got up, went over to his desk, and, unlocking a drawer, took out a small black leather book. There were a hundred and sixty thousand pounds at his bank which could be realized in a few days, and an almost equal amount in securities in a safe deposit which he rented. These would take a little longer to transform into fluid cash. He picked up a pencil and made a rapid calculation. Altogether he had about three hundred and fifty thousand pounds, enough for a man to live in luxury abroad. The thing to do was to convert it into diamonds. They were easily carried.

He had a bath and a shave, dressed with his usual care, and went out to seek an interview with his bank manager.

* * *

'I should like,' said Mr. Foxlow with respectful determination, 'ter give me notice.'

Mr. Benstead, who had just returned from banking the previous evening's takings at the cinema, looked at his foreman in surprise. 'Why, what's the matter, Foxlow?' he inquired. 'Aren't you satisfied?'

'It ain't that, sir. I've got a sister wot 'as a cottage in the country, an' 'er 'usband 'as just died, an' she wants me ter go an' live with 'er, bein' lonely, like. I can easy get a job there. There's a factory close by, an' — '

'When do you want to leave?' cut in Mr. Benstead.

'Well, it's a week on either side, ain't it?' said the foreman. 'So I'd like ter go on this comin' Sat'day, if it's all the same ter you, sir.'

'All right,' agreed Mr. Benstead, and the foreman left the office and returned to his duties.

His usefulness at the Mammoth Cinema, he thought, was over, and he would be very glad indeed to give up the irksome role he had adopted for so many weary weeks.

22

Colonel Hautboy Prepares
for Emergencies

Colonel Hautboy, immaculately dressed and outwardly the picture of prosperous contentment, turned into Hatton Garden and walked slowly along until he came to the entrance to the office he sought. Going up the narrow stairs, he stopped before a door on the second landing, tapped, and entered the outer office of Mr. Stiegmann. A shabby clerk escorted him into the inner sanctum and into the presence of Mr. Stiegmann, a suave and polite man who was looking forward to a profitable deal.

'I got your telephone message, Colonel Hautboy,' said Stiegmann. 'You're rather lucky, as a matter fact. We have just received a parcel of diamonds from Amsterdam containing some really beautiful stones — *beautiful* stones. I think you will find they're just what you're looking for.'

'I hope so,' said Hautboy. 'I should like to inspect them.'

Stiegmann rose from his desk with difficulty. He was a very short, fat little man whose legs seemed too diminutive and slender for his obese body. He opened a safe and took out a tray lined with black velvet upon which sparkled an array of diamonds — thirty of the finest stones Hautboy had seen for a long time.

'Examine them,' said Stiegmann, supplying him with a powerful lens. 'Aren't they beauties? I tell you, sir, that I have had many stones through my hands, but never any that were finer than these.' He rubbed his hands in mild ecstasy.

Hautboy examined them carefully and methodically. He eventually selected a dozen of the larger, which he put to one side. 'I'll take those,' he remarked, pushing the tray aside.

'You're an excellent judge, sir. You've chosen the pick of the bunch.'

'How much do I owe you?'

Stiegmann, after some rapid figuring

on his blotting-pad, named a price. It was a very large sum indeed, but Hautboy thought it was fair. He paid in notes from a large wad he took from his breast pocket.

'I'll have the stones parcelled up for you,' began Mr. Stiegmann, but Hautboy shook his head.

'No need to bother,' he said, producing a small leather bag. He scooped up the diamonds and dropped them into it, stowing it away in his waistcoat pocket. 'I shall probably be wanting more in a week or so,' he said as he took his leave. 'If you should have anything really good, ring me up and let me know.'

He shook hands with the diamond dealer and took his departure. Coming out into Hatton Garden, he almost knocked over Mr. Budd.

'Well, now, fancy meetin' you,' remarked the big man in apparent surprise. 'Bin buyin' a few diamond mines, Colonel?'

Hautboy was for a moment disconcerted, and then recovered his usual aplomb. 'One or two stones,' he replied. 'A birthday present for a friend.'

'Nice ter be able to give people expensive presents,' remarked Mr. Budd. 'You must be doin' very well.'

'Things aren't so bad.'

'Goin' back ter The Talkin' Parrot?' inquired Mr. Budd. 'I'll walk along with yer, if you don't mind bein' seen with a p'liceman.'

'Why should I?' said Hautboy sharply.

'Might start a lot of rumours. People might think you was pinched.'

Colonel Hautboy laughed, but it was not a very convincing laugh. 'Such a supposition would be ridiculous,' he declared. 'There's no reason on earth why I should be pinched, as you call it.'

Mr. Budd shook his head. 'Some people get funny ideas without havin' a reason. I've often thought I'd like ter buy diamonds, but o' course I'm not rich enough fer anythin' of the sort. It seems ter me a nice 'andy sort o' way of investin' yer money, though — partic'larly for anyone what wants to leave the country quickly.'

'What do you mean?' asked Hautboy quickly. 'Are you suggesting that I — '

'You?' said Mr. Budd in innocent surprise. 'Now 'ow could I 'ave been talkin' about you, Colonel? What would make you want ter leave the country in an 'urry?'

'Nothing,' snapped Hautboy.

'O' course it wouldn't. You've got a nice profitable business in that club o' yours. Some o' the richest people in the land are reg'lar customers of yours, so I'm told. Naturally you wouldn't want ter leave all that. No, I was thinkin' o' crim'nals. Now with them sort o' people, you never can tell. They're always anxious ter be able to slip off quick, an' diamonds 'ud be just the thing for them. Easy to carry, an' easy to turn back into cash.'

'Very likely,' said Hautboy. 'Yes, I should think you're probably right.' He was feeling a little ruffled. Was this sleepy-eyed man suspicious, or was he just drivelling on for the sake of saying something? He could gather no clue from Mr. Budd's expression, which was even more bovine than usual.

'It's a queer thing how stupid some crim'nals can be,' continued the big man.

'You'd be surprised. Now you wouldn't think that anybody 'ud try an' murder me, would you?'

'I don't call that stupid — from the criminal's point of view, of course,' Hautboy hastily corrected himself.

'It's stupid because it gives somethin' away. It tells me that I must be gettin' dangerous to the person concerned, an' *that* means I'm on the right track. D'yer see? But that's something you'll never get a crook to realize. He don't understand that every move he makes to safeguard 'imself is only givin' something away. Supplyin' just another small link in the chain of evidence against 'im.' He sighed wearily. 'Yer catch most of 'em because they won't leave well alone. If they'd just do nuthin' . . . But they won't, an' I suppose we ought ter be grateful — it makes 'em all the easier to catch.'

'Very . . . very interesting,' said Hautboy. 'Have you discovered anything more about the murder of that poor woman — what was her name? Pauline Rivers?'

'*Paula* Rivers,' corrected Mr. Budd

gently. 'She was mixed up in this drug traffickin'.'

'How do you know that?'

'Information received,' answered Mr. Budd vaguely. 'I expect you'd know somethin' about that.'

'About what?'

'About this drug traffickin'. Runnin' a place like The Talkin' Parrot 'ud be bound to bring it under yer nose, so to speak.'

'I'm afraid you're mistaken,' said Hautboy. 'Nothing like that goes on at The Talking Parrot. Anyone who attempted to peddle drugs in my establishment would get short shrift, I can assure you. I've always prided myself that The Talking Parrot is the most well-conducted club in London.'

'I'll admit that you've been very careful,' agreed Mr. Budd, and Hautboy wondered exactly what he meant by that rather cryptic phrase.

The stout superintendent left Hautboy outside The Talking Parrot and made his way back to Scotland Yard. Leek was waiting for him with a report on Lord Penstemmon, but before attending to it

Mr. Budd got through on the house telephone to Colonel Blair.

'Can I have two men detailed to shadow Colonel Hautboy, sir?' he said. 'I've got an idea he's contemplatin' a getaway.'

'What makes you think that?' asked the assistant commissioner.

'He's buyin' diamonds, sir,' said Mr. Budd. 'An' when a feller like 'Autboy starts buyin' diamonds, it usually means one thing.'

'We've got nothing against him,' said Colonel Blair doubtfully. 'That club of his is run strictly in accordance with the law.'

'We've got nuthin' against 'im *yet*,' corrected Mr. Budd, 'but we may 'ave plenty before very long. I think 'e's in this drug traffickin' pretty deep, an' closely concerned with the murder of the gal Rivers. I don't want 'im to have a chance of slippin' through our fingers.'

'All right,' said the assistant commissioner after a slight pause. 'You can have your two men, but for the Lord's sake be careful. If Hautboy finds out he's being watched and likes to be nasty about it, we're laying ourselves open to a lot of trouble.'

''E won't make any trouble, sir,' said Mr. Budd confidently. 'An' there's no reason why 'e should find out — not if they're clever.'

He hung up the receiver and turned his attention to Leek's report. There was little in it he had not known before. Penstemmon was in a pretty bad financial mess. His creditors were legion, and he appeared to owe money everywhere. At quite a number of hotels and clubs he was barred. It was fairly safe to conclude that his word could not be relied on. It was not he who had introduced Paula Rivers to The Talking Parrot. The mistake he had made about her colouring had shown that he was lying. Somebody had forced him to say he was her escort, and that somebody had probably been Colonel Hautboy. But who had actually taken her to the club? Who was it that Hautboy and Penstemmon were shielding? Unless it was someone who was actually concerned with her murder, there would be no need for it. It was not an offence to take a pretty woman to a nightclub.

Somewhere in the background, pulling all the strings, was an as yet unknown person. Someone who gave the orders and did the planning. The maker of bullets for others to fire. Mr. Budd had sensed something of the sort from the beginning. Was it the mysterious whispering woman who flitted elusively through the whole affair?

He sighed, lit a cigar, and leaned back in his chair. 'I've got another job for yer,' he said suddenly, looking up at Leek. 'Now don't look as though you was goin' ter be executed. Work's good for yer. It keeps you from broodin' on 'ow miserable yer life is.'

'Nobody can ever say I'm afraid o' work,' said the sergeant.

'If they was truthful, they'd say you was terrified,' snapped Mr. Budd.

'I don't know why you should always be gettin' at me,' remonstrated Leek feebly. 'I always does me best.'

'Well, this is a nice easy job, an' all you've got ter do is try an' keep awake over it. You know Eileen Rivers?'

'The dead gal's sister?' said Leek, nodding. 'Rather a nice gal, I thought.'

'You keep your mind on your work,' said Mr. Budd severely.

'I wasn't thinkin' what *you* was thinkin',' said Leek indignantly.

'I should hope not. Now, what I want you to do is keep an eye on this Eileen Rivers. Let me know where she goes an' who she sees.'

'Why? Do you think — '

'I've got a hunch that it may lead somewhere,' said Mr. Budd dreamily. 'You needn't bother durin' the day. It's in the evenin' an' durin' the night that I want ter know what she does.'

'When do I sleep?'

'Most of the time,' snarled Mr. Budd.

'I mean — '

'I know what you mean,' sighed the big man. 'You can sleep all day if you like. Only, if that woman goes anywhere durin' the evenin', see that you're wide awake enough to foller 'er.'

23

Sergeant Leek Makes a Discovery

Sergeant Leek prepared to carry out the task which Mr. Budd had assigned to him without any great enthusiasm. It was a job he disliked intensely, and it was one that always seemed to fall to his lot.

After a rest and a meal, he made his way to Eden Street and sought for a place of vantage from which he could keep a watch on the Rivers house without making himself too conspicuous. It was not very easy to do this. The little street, he thought, was particularly unsuitable for this purpose. The rows of small houses, their front doors opening directly onto the pavement, offered nothing in the way of cover.

He walked slowly up the street on one side and down again on the other. On the corner was a small general shop that was now closed. It had a recessed doorway which, he concluded a little unhappily, was the only possible place. Here, at least, he would not be visible from the window of the Rivers house, although he might become an object of suspicion and interest to other inhabitants of the street.

He took an evening paper from his pocket and began to study it. He read every word on the front page, then carefully folded the paper inside out, and began to read the second page. He had almost finished that when it began to rain — a few isolated drops at first, and then faster and faster until the pavements and the road were shining.

Leek sighed and turned up the collar of his shabby mackintosh. It looked as though he was going to have an unpleasant time of it. Why, he thought with sudden self-pity, did it always have to rain whenever he was on a job like this?

He continued to read the rest of the paper. The rain was falling heavily now, with a steady persistence that looked as though it was likely to continue indefinitely, and with it had come a cold wind. It blew in gusts round the corner, driving the rain into the doorway of the shop.

Leek shivered. There was no sign of life at the Rivers house. No sign of life in the dingy street at all. The few children who had been playing in the road when he had first arrived had disappeared. His spirits sank lower and lower. The whole prospect was depressing.

He took out his handkerchief and blew his nose. Perhaps it would be a good idea if he moved off for a bit. He had been in the doorway for a long time, and he didn't want to draw too much attention to his presence. He walked up the street again, lingered for a minute or two at the other end, and then came back. It was more than likely that he was having all this trouble for nothing. Eileen Rivers, if she was even at home, was probably spending the evening indoors. On a night like this had turned out to be, she would be a fool to leave the comfort of her home. He thought nobody would unless they had to. He knew where *he'd* be if he had the choice.

A car turned in at the other end of the road and came swiftly toward him. It was an expensive, high-powered car — a Lagonda. It slowed halfway and pulled up outside the Rivers house. A man got out and knocked at the door. Jimmy Redfern.

Here was a pretty kettle of fish, thought Leek in dismay. If Eileen Rivers was going anywhere in that car, he had as much hope of finding out where she was going as if he was on the moon.

The door was opened. Redfern said something to somebody Leek couldn't see, and then beckoned to somebody in the car. Another man got out and joined him, and they both went into the house.

The melancholy sergeant thought quickly. The main road was only a short distance away, and there was just a chance he might pick up a taxi. It was true that while he was gone they might come out of the house and drive away, but he would lose them anyway. It was worth the risk. He hurried away as fast as his long, thin legs would take him.

There was plenty of traffic in the main road but no sign of a taxi. He walked rapidly along towards the Mammoth Cinema; and as he reached it he was lucky enough to see a cab set down two people outside the entrance, and ran forward to secure it. Hastily he explained to the cab driver who he was and what he wanted.

'Awl right, mate,' said the man, ''op in.'

Leek did so gratefully. It was pleasant to sit back in sheltered comfort from the cold rain. They reached the top of Eden Street just in time to see Eileen Rivers, Jimmy Redfern and the other man come out and get into the Lagonda.

'I want you to follow that car,' said Leek, leaning forward and speaking through the partly opened window in the partition behind the driver.

'I'll do me best, mate,' said the driver. 'But this old bus ain't jet-propelled, you know, an' that blinkin' car's a Lagonda. If it puts on any speed, it can leave us standin' still.'

The Lagonda moved away from the kerb. It slid swiftly up the length of Eden Street and turned the corner, and the taxi with Leek huddled in the corner of his seat went after it. The driver had obviously underestimated the cab, since while the car he was following put on speed when it reached the main road, he was able to keep about two hundred yards behind it with comparative ease. It was true that it was by no means all out, but Leek was banking on the fact that it would not reach that stage.

It was a long chase that led them out into open country, and more than once they almost lost their quarry when the Lagonda put on a burst of speed.

''Ow much further, mate?' asked the driver as they sped through Dorking. 'I'm gettin' pretty low on petrol.'

'I don't know,' Leek replied. 'But I shouldn't think it could be much further.'

'Well I 'ope not, or we're goin' to get stranded. Not that I mind. It wouldn't be the first time I've slept in the old cab, an' I don't s'pose it'd be the last.'

They came to a stretch of country road with hedges and open fields and a few houses. The Lagonda slowed down as it rounded a bend; and they were just in time, as they followed it, to see it turn into the driveway of one of the houses. The cab driver ran his cab a few yards past this opening and pulled up.

''Ere we are, mate,' he said, 'with about 'alf a gallon o' juice left in the perishin' tank. Wot do we do now?'

'You stop 'ere,' said Leek, getting out. 'Pretend to be tinkerin' with your engine if anybody comes along. I'm goin' to 'ave a look round.'

He walked back along the road to the drive entrance. Looking in, he could see the Lagonda drawn up in front of a pillared porch that belonged to a fairly large house. Drawing back out of sight, Leek pondered over what he should do next. Should he explore further and try and find out what had brought Eileen Rivers and Jimmy Redfern to this place, and who lived here? Or should he find the nearest telephone and report what he had discovered to Mr. Budd?

He decided that this latter course was, perhaps, the better. There was very little he could do by prowling round the outside of the house; and if he were seen by the inmates, it might do a great deal of harm. They would guess that the Lagonda had been followed and be put instantly on their guard.

He went back to the cab. 'I want you to take me to a telephone,' he said. 'An' if you can find a garridge, you'd better fill up with petrol.'

'O.K., mate,' said the accommodating driver. 'We'd best go back the way we come.'

They found both a telephone and a garage just outside Dorking. While the driver was getting his tank filled, Leek put through a call to Mr. Budd. He rang the stout superintendent's little house in Streatham, guessing that by now he would have left the Yard. Mr. Budd's slow, husky voice answered the call, and Leek explained what had happened.

'Good,' said Mr. Budd. 'You've done very well. Now just you stop where you are until I get there, an' then you can show me this place. Yer needn't bother any more about the gal Rivers an' 'er friends. If they leave before I get there, it don't matter.'

'I'm feelin' a bit 'ungry,' said Leek. 'There's a cafe in Dorking called the Blue Kettle — couldn't you pick me up there?'

Rather to the sergeant's surprise, Mr. Budd readily agreed and without any of his usual caustic and sarcastic comments. Leek concluded that he must be very pleased indeed.

He paid off the cab driver and went in search of the Blue Kettle, which he found closed for the night. There appeared to be no other restaurant that was open either, and Leek foresaw a long, hungry wait.

Wearily, since there was nothing else to do to pass the time, he began to stroll rather dejectedly about, and presently came upon a small public house. Although he did not drink anything alcoholic, he thought that he might be able to get a sandwich and went in. The bar was not very crowded, and he ordered a lime-juice and soda. There were no sandwiches, but he got a couple of cheese rolls, which he munched with relish. There was a vacant stool by the bar, and on this he perched himself, deciding that he would stay there until it was near time to meet Mr. Budd.

It was quite dark when he left the pub and made his way back to the Blue

Kettle. There was no sign as yet of the big man, and he took up a position in the doorway and waited.

It was the longest wait he could remember. It seemed hours and hours before he saw the lights of a car coming towards him, and recognized the peculiar noise it was making for Mr. Budd's ancient machine. It drew up with a protesting squeal of brakes, and the big superintendent beckoned to him.

''Aven't been long, 'ave I?' he said as the sergeant shambled over. 'Surprisin' what this car can do at a pinch. You 'op in an' show me where this place is.'

Leek couldn't be said exactly to 'hop', but he got in beside his superior. 'You go on down this road an' then you turns to the right,' he said. 'After that, you — '

'That'll do to be goin' on with,' said Mr. Budd. 'You can tell me the rest as we go.'

He seemed to be in a high good humour. There was not a trace of the irritability that Leek had to put up with so often. The sergeant concluded that everything must be going very well indeed.

They reached the house at last, and Mr. Budd pulled up at the entrance to the drive and got out. 'Come on,' he said, to Leek's surprise. 'We'll pay 'em a call.'

'Do you mean you're goin' to go up to the door an' knock?' asked the sergeant.

The big man nodded. 'That's it. Everythin' open an' above-board.'

'There's the car,' said Leek as they walked up the drive. 'They're still 'ere.'

'Good. That's goin' ter make things a lot easier.'

They came to the porch. The stout superintendent stopped for a moment. Then he lumbered up the shallow steps, fumbled for the knocker, and gave a reverberating rat-tat.

24

George Nicholls's Uncle

Nothing happened. From inside the house there was no sound at all.

Mr. Budd knocked again, louder and more urgently. Again there was a long interval of silence; and then, just as he was about to knock for the third time, there came the muffled sound of an approaching footstep and the door was opened. A man in the conventional black garb of an upper servant peered out at them.

'What is it?' he inquired.

Mr. Budd cleared his throat. 'Could you tell me who lives 'ere?' he asked. 'This is Mr. Muir's residence,' replied the manservant. 'Mr. Jonathan Muir.'

'Could I see Mr. Muir?' inquired Mr. Budd.

'Well, I don't know . . . ' The man hesitated. 'Mr. Muir is engaged at the moment with some friends. Who shall I say it is?'

Mr. Budd took out his wallet, extracted a card, and held it out. 'Just take 'im that an' say I should like to 'ave a word with 'im.'

The manservant took the card, glanced at it, and gave Mr. Budd a quick, sharp look. 'Will you please wait,' he said, and closed the door.

'Who's this feller Muir?' asked Leek.

Mr. Budd shook his head. 'I don't know no more'n you do. Maybe we'll find out soon.'

'You don't suppose this feller's goin' ter give anythin' away, do yer? Not now 'e knows who you are.'

'He's got ter talk, ain't 'e?'

'What good's that? 'E can say anythin'. I don't think you've 'andled this quite right . . . '

'Oh, you don't, eh?' snarled Mr. Budd. 'I s'pose you'd 'ave disguised yerself in a false beard an' pretended yer was the Archbishop o' Timbuctoo!'

'I'd've been a bit more subtle. I wouldn't've let on who I was.'

'He'd've known after one look at yer feet,' retorted Mr. Budd. 'Now shut up. 'Ere comes someone.'

It was the manservant. He opened the door and politely invited them to come in. He led them across the well-furnished hall, opened a door on the right, and ushered them into a small room that was empty. 'Mr. Muir will see you in a few minutes,' he said, and left them.

Mr. Budd looked about. There was evidence of wealth and taste here. The carpet was thick and expensive, the furniture old and good; and the few pictures on the walls, although he knew nothing about such things, looked valuable.

The door opened, and a stout middle-aged man with a bald head came in, carrying Mr. Budd's card in his fingers. 'You wished to see me — er — Superintendent?' he inquired with a slightly puzzled intonation.

'You Mr. Muir?' asked Mr. Budd.

'Yes.'

'You the tenant of this house?'

'I am the owner.' Mr. Muir's fattish face was a little astonished: 'I cannot understand why you have come to see me.'

'Just to ask you a few questions, sir. You are acquainted, I believe, with a Miss Eileen Rivers an' a Mr. Redfern.'

'Most certainly I am,' broke in the bald man. 'They are, as a matter of fact, here now. I cannot see, however, what concern this is of the police.'

'You'd be surprised, sir, if you knew the things which concerns the police,' said Mr. Budd. 'May I ask 'ow long you've known these people?'

'I met them for the first time a few nights ago. They're friends of my nephew, and he brought them.'

'Your nephew, sir?' said Mr. Budd inquiringly.

'Mr. George Nicholls.'

Mr. Budd felt a sudden acute sense of disappointment. Was that all it was, after all? He had hoped and expected to make an important discovery, and this was all it had ended in. What was more ordinary than that George Nicholls should visit his uncle and bring his friends with him? Nothing, except ... there was one strange thing. If this was all, why had Mrs. Rivers been sent for in the early hours of the morning?

'Oh, I see, sir,' murmured Mr. Budd. 'Mr. Nicholls is your nephew?'

Muir nodded. He still looked a little puzzled. 'May I inquire the reason for these questions?' he asked.

'Well, sir, I'm in charge of the investigation into the murder of Miss Eileen Rivers's sister.'

'What has that to do with me?'

'We were rather curious to know what Miss Rivers, Mr. Redfern an' Mr. Nicholls were doin' 'ere.'

'Well, you know now. I'm afraid that it has not been of much assistance to you in your investigation. If there's nothing further, I should be glad to get back to my guests.'

Mr. Budd took his departure with as good a grace as he could muster. He felt that the interview had been decidedly disappointing.

'What do we do now?' asked Leek as the stout superintendent climbed ponderously into his ancient car.

'We find the perlice station,' grunted Mr. Budd. 'I'd like to have a word with the inspector in charge.'

'We didn't learn much there, did we?' said Leek, jerking his narrow head towards the house.

'Not enough to notice, but I'm not at all sure there isn't somethin' we ought to learn.'

'D'you think the old man was phoney?'

'Where d'yer pick up these American expressions?' said Mr. Budd disapprovingly.

'The pitchers. I like a good crook film, 'specially 'Umphrey Bogart. Now there's a feller for you.'

'I don't want 'im,' snapped Mr. Budd. 'Now, s'pose yer keep quiet an' let me think.'

Leek sighed. The disappointing interview with Mr. Jonathan Muir had made the big man irritable. He was likely to get very cross indeed unless he were humoured. The melancholy sergeant stared out of the side window and remained mute.

They found the police station and pulled up opposite the blue lamp. Mr.

Budd entered the charge room and introduced himself to the desk sergeant. 'I'd like to see the inspector or superintendent in charge,' he said. 'I want to make an inquiry.'

The desk sergeant called a constable, and Mr. Budd was taken to the inspector's office. The inspector was a thin, raw-boned man with grizzled hair.

'What d'you know about a man called Jonathan Muir, who lives about a mile an' an 'alf away in a house named Woodstock?' asked Mr. Budd, coming straight to the object of his visit.

The inspector raised his eyebrows. 'I know quite a lot about Mr. Muir,' he said. ''E's on the council an' 'e's a J.P. You can't 'ave anything against 'im.'

'I didn't say I 'ad,' said Mr. Budd. 'Tell me all you know about 'im.'

The inspector considered. He was a slow and methodical man and was not to be hurried. 'Well, sir,' he began, ''e's a very rich man and well liked in the district. When the tragedy 'appened, there was scarcely anybody what didn't feel deeply for 'im.'

'What was this tragedy?' interrupted Mr. Budd sharply.

'It was 'is daughter,' replied the inspector. 'Committed suicide, she did. It was a very sad business. Took an overdose of some sleepin' stuff — heroin, I think they call it. The maid-servant found 'er dead in 'er bed in the mornin'.'

'When did this 'appen?'

'About ten months ago. Poor Mr. Muir was very cut up. I saw 'im at the inquest, an' you'd never 'ave thought a man could change so much in such a short time. 'Is daughter was all 'e 'ad, of course. 'Is wife died three or four years ago.'

'Was 'is nephew at the inquest?'

'No, I don't think so,' said the inspector. 'I didn't know 'e 'ad a nephew.'

'Never mind,' said Mr. Budd. 'Tell me some more about this suicide of 'is daughter's. Why did she kill 'erself?'

The inspector couldn't say. No satisfactory reason had come to light at the inquest. 'It's my belief,' he said, 'that there was some man or other at the bottom of it — though, mind you, I've no proof. But she was a flighty piece of goods, always out until all hours of the night, dancing and drinking in these London clubs.'

'What was 'er name?' asked Mr. Budd.

'Jacqueline Muir. She 'ad a friend, as mad-brained as herself. Now, let me see, what was 'er name? Queer kind of name it was . . . ' He screwed up his face in an effort of memory. 'Trudi, that was it. Miss Trudi Rhodes.'

'Does she live in the district?' inquired Mr. Budd.

The inspector shook his head. 'No — somewhere in London. She were often down 'ere, though, staying with Jacqueline Muir.'

Mr. Budd put several more questions, but the inspector had apparently exhausted all the information he possessed on the subject, and the big man went back to his car.

He had learned something that might be important, and he was silent and thoughtful as he drove back to London. Jacqueline Muir had died from an overdose of heroin. Had she been a victim of the drugs racket, or was it merely a coincidence? He thought not. Perhaps this woman, Trudi Rhodes, would supply him with further information. He made up his mind to find out her address and interview her as soon as possible.

25

Eileen Changes Her Job

Mr. Budd put his plan into execution first thing the following morning. It was not a difficult matter to find Miss Trudi Rhodes's address. He tried the telephone directory and was lucky. She lived in a big block of flats in Knightsbridge, Caversham Mansions, and Mr. Budd was taken up in a smooth-running lift to the fifth floor.

A maid answered the door to his ring. She was a sour-faced woman in black who regarded him suspiciously.

'Is Miss Rhodes in?' he inquired.

The maid sniffed. 'Miss Rhodes is in bed an' can't be disturbed. What do you want?'

'I want a word with your mistress,' said Mr. Budd, holding out a card. 'I won't keep 'er long, but it's important.'

The maid took the card, looked at it

and sniffed again. Mr. Budd concluded that it was a nervous affliction.

'The perlice, eh?' she said. 'What's it all about?'

'I'm afraid I can only tell that to Miss Rhodes,' replied Mr. Budd.

The woman looked at him. Her eyes were small and very dark. 'All right, I'll see if she'll see you. You'd better wait there.'

She left him standing on the doormat and closed the door. She was gone for such a long time that Mr. Budd was beginning to think she had gone for good. Just as he was considering ringing again, she came back.

'She'll see you. Come this way, will you?' She crossed the small hall, opened a door, and ushered him into a bedroom which was tastefully furnished and very untidy.

Amid a sea of silken pillows a woman lay in the bed. Mr. Budd thought she wasn't really very old, but she looked it. Her face was haggard, and the mass of dark hair that fell over her shoulders was lustreless. She looked at him with dull, drowsy eyes, and her voice when she spoke was husky and listless.

'What do you want?' she asked.

'I'm given to understand, miss,' said Mr. Budd, standing a little awkwardly at the foot of the bed, 'that you were friendly with a Miss Muir.'

'You mean Jacky?' She spoke without interest. 'Yes, I was.'

'We're rather interested in the young lady's death.'

'Oh, really.' Trudi Rhodes shifted her head languidly, and her expression was one of supreme boredom. 'Why?'

'Well, it seems queer that she should've committed suicide without a reason.'

'I'm quite sure she didn't.'

'You mean there *was* a reason?'

'No,' she answered, 'I mean I'm sure she didn't commit suicide. It was an accident.'

'But the verdict at the inquest was suicide, wasn't it?'

'Oh yes. But of course it was just nonsense. Jacky took an overdose of heroin. She probably didn't know what she was doing. I expect she was lit up when she took it.'

'Do you mean she was drunk?' demanded Mr. Budd bluntly.

'No, drugged,' replied Trudi calmly. 'She used to take heroin, you know. Or didn't you?'

'She was a drug addict, was she?'

'Oh yes. I used to tell her how silly she was, but of course she wouldn't listen. You can't reason with people like that.'

Mr. Budd thought that it would be difficult for Miss Rhodes to 'reason' with anybody. He thought, also, that she was not entirely unused to drugs either. He said: 'Was her father aware that she took drugs?'

'Oh yes, he was very upset about it.'

'An' where did she get these drugs?'

'I'm sure I don't know. I asked her once, but of course she wouldn't tell me.'

'She used to go to nightclubs quite a lot, didn't she?'

'Oh yes.' Trudi stifled a yawn delicately. 'But of course, we all do. How else can one amuse oneself?'

'Was she a member of The Talking Parrot?'

'Of course.' She raised her thin pencilled brows a fraction, as though it were ridiculous for anybody to ask such a foolish question. 'Everybody's a member of The Talking Parrot. It's one of the most amusing places in town.'

'Could she 'ave got 'er supply of drugs there?' asked Mr. Budd, watching her face keenly.

'It's possible, isn't it?' she answered without any change of expression at all. 'Such a mixed crowd get into these places nowadays that really *anything* is possible.'

The maid came in with a tray of tea. She looked at Mr. Budd, sniffed, and set the tray down on the table beside her mistress's bed.

'Pour it out, Miranda, there's a lamb,' said Trudi wearily.

The sour-faced maid obeyed with the deft efficiency of long practice.

'Is that all, Mr. — er — ?' Trudi took the cup with a hand that trembled slightly and sipped the hot tea. 'I really can't tell you anything more about Jacky. She was a sweet woman. I miss her terribly.'

'You knew 'er father, too?' said Mr. Budd gently.

'Oh yes. I don't think he approved of me . . . I'm afraid he rather thought it was my fault. Quite ridiculous, of course. I had no influence at all over Jacky.'

I wonder, thought Mr. Budd. Aloud he said: 'We're very anxious to find out where Miss Muir was gettin' these drugs from.'

'I can't help you, I'm afraid. Another cup of tea, Miranda, please. Naturally she never told me. I knew she took them, of course. Her father asked me the same question. He was quite rude about it, but I knew he was too upset to realize what he was saying. Really, I don't know anything more about it. Poor Jacky. I was frightfully cut up, of course, when I heard what had happened to her. Such a devastating thing . . . Miranda, give me a cigarette.'

Mr. Budd took his leave. It was quite useless expecting any information from this woman. Even half-doped, as she undoubtedly was, she was still far too clever to give anything away. As he drove his ancient car towards the Mammoth Cinema, he was certain of one thing: Trudi Rhodes knew perfectly well where Jacqueline Muir had obtained her drugs. From the same source, he was willing to bet, that she got her own.

★　★　★

Mr. Emanuel Benstead came back after banking the previous day's takings, hung up his hat and coat, and sat down behind the desk in his small office. It was half-past eleven. The Mammoth Cinema would not open its doors to the public for another hour and three-quarters. Faintly to his ears came the strains of the Wurlitzer organ. Harry Stanton was practising a new programme.

Benstead lit a cigarette and inhaled the smoke gratefully. Ever since the death of Paula Rivers, he had been a greatly worried man. He had not yet succeeded in replacing her; and although he had promoted Grace Singer to the position of chief cashier, he was still short-staffed. And at the end of that week Mr. Foxlow would be leaving.

He had put a slide on the screen advertising for a cashier and a chief of staff, but so far without much result. He had had one or two applicants, but the wages he was allowed to offer were so small that they were not interested. How could you expect anyone to undertake an exacting job with long hours when they could get more money doing almost anything else? It just wasn't reasonable. But reasonable or not, staff had to be found.

He was puzzling over this problem when somebody tapped at the door of his office. 'Come in,' he called, and Eileen Rivers appeared. She was so changed that he scarcely recognized her at first. Her whole appearance had acquired a smartness that was very different to the drab, colourless woman he remembered when her sister had been alive.

'I hope I haven't disturbed you, Mr. Benstead,' she said, 'but are you still looking for a cashier?'

'Yes,' answered Benstead.

'Well, I've given up my job, and I was

wondering if you'd give me a trial. I've never done any actual box office work, but I'm quite a good cashier, and I do know how to work the ticket machines — Paula showed me one day.'

'I'll be pleased to engage you, Miss Rivers,' said Benstead, delighted at this unexpected stroke of luck. 'When can you start?'

'As soon as you like. Today, if you wish.'

'That will be fine. I'll arrange for Miss Singer to show you how to take the numbers and the ticket stock book. There's really nothing difficult about it. We're not very busy, as a rule, in the afternoon, and by the evening you ought to be able to take over box B on your own. I'll be around in case you get into any trouble. Mostly a matter of speed in giving change.'

'I think I shall be able to manage it,' said Eileen.

'I'm sure you will. We open today at one-fifteen. Will you be here at one sharp?' Eileen promised that she would, and left the office. Outside, Jimmy

Redfern and George Nicholls were waiting for her.

'Well?' said Jimmy, and she nodded.

'I've got the job,' she said. 'I'm starting today at one o'clock. Oh Jimmy, I'm . . . scared.'

'I don't think you ought to do it,' said Jimmy. 'I'm dead against it. I told you so at the start.'

'But it's the only way.'

'I don't see why *you* have to take the risk,' put in Nicholls. 'I think it was too much to ask you to do.'

'I'm the only one who *could* do it,' Eileen insisted.

'If anything goes wrong,' said Jimmy, 'I'll never forgive myself!'

'Don't be silly,' she said. 'Nothing *is* going wrong.'

'I hope not,' said Nicholls. 'Well, come along. If you've got to get back here at one, you'd better come and have some lunch.'

26

Jimmy Redfern Is Worried

Eileen Rivers slipped into the job of second cashier at the Mammoth Cinema fairly easily. She had a good head for figures, and under the expert guidance of Grace Singer soon mastered the technicalities of the automatic ticket machines and the system of replacing tickets from stock. By the end of her first afternoon, she was sufficiently expert to take over box B on her own when it was opened at six-thirty for the evening.

'Don't let them rush you,' said Mr. Benstead as he checked her starting numbers on the machine. 'Take your time.'

She was a little nervous when the queue grew large, but she forced herself to keep cool and managed very well. By the time the last performance was underway and everybody was in, however, she was feeling desperately tired.

'Nearly over, dear,' said Grace as they made up the returns and checked over the money. 'You've been wonderful. What's the total? A hundred and four pounds sixteen and eightpence? We're two pounds ten over. How did that happen, I wonder? Perhaps I've made a mistake. Count up the money again, will you, dear?'

Eileen went quickly through the two wads of pound- and ten-shilling notes and checked the contents of the silver and copper bags. 'You were right,' she said. 'We're two pounds ten shillings over.'

'Oh dear,' said Grace. 'Now we shall have to check the returns all through again, and I wanted to get away early.'

'Surely it doesn't matter if we're over?'

'Oh yes, it does, dear. It's as bad as being under. It shows there's a mistake somewhere, and head office will find it. Here it is! Mr. Benstead gave us two-pound-ten's worth of cigarettes and we've forgotten to enter them. There! Now it's all right.' She picked up the return book. 'You bring the money, dear, will you?' she said, opening the door of box A and hurrying off to Mr. Benstead's office.

Eileen followed with the money, and Benstead checked it with the return sheet and signed it. He tore out the top sheet and one of the two carbon copies, which Miss Singer hastily put in a printed envelope addressed to head office. She stamped it and bade them good night.

'Well, how do you like being a cinema cashier, Miss Rivers?' asked the manager as he stuffed the notes and bags of money into a blue linen bank bag and locked it away in the safe.

'Very much,' she answered.

'You've done well — very well, indeed.'

'I don't think it's very difficult,' she said with a smile.

He shook his head. 'You'd be surprised how few can do it. I've had experienced cashiers who've fallen down badly. It's the speed that gets them — when we're really busy, I mean. They just can't cope with it.'

'It does get you a bit dizzy at first,' she admitted, 'but you soon get used to it.'

She said good night and went out, passing Mr. Foxlow in the vestibule. Jimmy Redfern was waiting outside, and she was surprised, for she had not expected him.

'Thought I'd see you home,' he said. 'What about coffee and a snack at Gina's? You must be hungry.'

She was more tired than anything else, but she wouldn't have refused for anything. 'That would be nice,' she said, and slipped her hand through his arm. She thought she felt a slight pressure from his arm, but it might only be imagination.

The snack bar was crowded, but they managed to find two stools and perched themselves at the counter. Jimmy ordered coffee and sandwiches, and while the order was being executed, offered her a cigarette.

'Well, how did it go?' he asked.

'Mr. Benstead said I did very well.'

'You'll look after yourself, won't you?' he said seriously. 'I've been terribly worried all day.'

'I don't see what can happen to me,'

she said, laughing, but she was pleased that he should be so concerned about her.

'Anything might. These people are desperate, Eileen; and if you find out their secret . . . Well, you know what happened to Paula.'

'Yes, but that was different. Paula let them know she'd found out.'

'They'll be watching you,' he warned. 'Don't kid yourself that they haven't guessed what you're there for. They'll be watching all the time!'

'If we only knew who 'they' were,' she murmured.

He nodded. 'That makes it worse. And more dangerous. They know you, but you don't know them. D'you think it's Benstead?'

'No. I don't think Mr. Benstead has got anything to do with it at all. I've got an idea, but . . . '

'What is it?' asked Jimmy.

She shook her head. 'I'm not telling you. I may be quite wrong. It was only something that I saw . . . There may be nothing in it.'

He tried to make her tell him, but she

wouldn't. 'I'd rather wait until I'm sure, Jimmy,' she said. 'It may be nothing at all. Here's the coffee.'

They finished the snack and he walked with her to Eden Street.

'Good night, Eileen,' he said. 'No, I won't come in. I'll be outside the Mammoth tomorrow night at the same time. And don't forget — take care of yourself.'

She watched him go up the street before she put her key in the lock. Halfway along, he looked back and waved. She let herself into the house with a glow in her heart. Jimmy, who had never seemed to know that she existed before, was interested.

Later that night, just before she got into bed, Eileen looked at herself in the mirror. What she saw startled her. She was completely different to the drab, homely, colourless woman she had been. The change was remarkable. It was wonderful what a shampoo and set and a little makeup could do. Or was it something more than that? There was an inner glow that shone out of her eyes and warmed the soft skin. She got into bed and fell asleep, contented and happy, and dreamed of Jimmy Redfern.

★ ★ ★

'I want you,' said Mr. Budd to the melancholy Leek, 'to go along to that 'ouse of Muir's an' keep an eye on it. You don't 'ave to get too close. Just keep watch on the entrance to the drive an' make a note of who goes in an' comes out. Understand?'

Leek understood, but the understanding didn't seem to make him too happy. 'All the time?' he asked.

'I'll send someone ter relieve yer an' yer can take it in turns. Make it four hours on an' four hours off. You'd better fix up at the perlice station fer meals in the canteen an' a camp bed so's you can sleep.'

'What good d'you think's comin' from it?'

'Well, candidly, I don't know,' confessed Mr. Budd. 'But I'm not satisfied about Muir. I'd like to know the real reason why all these people — Eileen Rivers, Redfern, an' this feller Nicholls — keep goin' there. There's somethin' fishy about it. Why should they 'ave fetched Mrs. Rivers in the early hours o' the mornin'? You can bet it wasn't for a social call.'

'That gal Eileen Rivers 'as got 'erself employed at the Mammoth Cinema,' said Leek. 'As second cashier.'

'Ow did you know that?' said Mr. Budd sharply.

'Longfoot rang up just before you came in. I forgot to tell you. Slipped out o' me mind until you mentioned it.'

'Now, I wonder why she's done that?' remarked Mr. Budd thoughtfully, pulling gently at one ear.

'Maybe she wanted a job.'

'She 'ad a job an' a good job,' grunted Mr. Budd. 'I'll bet she was gettin' more money than she'll get at the cinema. Hm, interestin' an' peculiar. You get off ter Dorkin'. I want to think . . . '

He settled himself in his chair behind his desk when the sergeant had gone and stared at the ceiling. Eileen Rivers was poking her head in the lion's den. Did she realize her danger? And what had prompted her to do it? Curiosity? Did she imagine that she could find out the truth about her sister's murder? Maybe that was her reason — but did she know what an appalling risk she was running?

If she *did* stumble on something, and these people found out, she'd go the same way as Paula. And what part was Muir playing in all this? Had he prevailed on her to take this job? Had these visits to the house on the outskirts of Dorking been the preliminary, leading to this? If this plan had been hatched there, what was the reason? Was Jonathan Muir trying to find out the reason behind his daughter's death? He had been aware that she was a drug addict, he must have been; so was he trying to find who had been supplying her? If so, Eileen Rivers was undertaking a dangerous mission. Her sister had played with fire and got fatally burnt. Mr. Budd hoped that Eileen would not suffer the same fate.

27

In the Void

Three days went slowly by. Eileen Rivers performed her duties quietly and efficiently and earned the praise of Mr. Benstead, while Mr. Foxlow continued his job as chief of staff and looked forward to the rapidly approaching moment when he could discard his irksome role forever and resume his own character for twenty-four hours a day. Grace Singer went about her work as usual and wondered what the future held in store for her. Colonel Hautboy continued to acquire diamonds and planned his getaway with methodical care; and Mr. Budd waited, watchful and vigilant, and quietly spun his web in the hope of entrapping the fly whose identity he did not know. Sergeant Leek, with the assistance of Detective Constable Brewer, kept a weary and so far profitless vigil on

Jonathan Muir's house and sent negative reports to his superior.

Eileen had been watchful, but she had seen nothing to confirm the vague suspicions she had mentioned to Jimmy Redfern. The ordinary routine of the cinema went on without anything to break the monotony. Until the evening of the third day.

It was a Thursday, which was early-closing day in the district, and at six-thirty they began to get busy. The Mammoth Cinema was showing a very good programme. Both the main feature and the second feature were excellent films, and by six-twenty there was a long queue for the cheaper seats and the circle was rapidly filling up.

Benstead darted about, in and out of the cinema, up the stairs to the circle and back, urging the usherettes to an unusual activity and keeping a check on the number of vacant seats. He managed in the midst of all this to find time to dash up to the storeroom and bring down a carton of cigarettes for sale at box A. Each of these cartons contained ten packets of twenty, and Benstead used to ration them out to one carton a night. When the ten packets were sold, which was usually fairly quickly, he would issue no more until the following evening. Eileen, through the glass side of box B, saw Grace Singer stack the packets of cigarettes on the bare space beside the polished top of the automatic ticket machine, within easy reach.

The circle was full by now, and there was a fairly large queue waiting, so that Eileen had nothing to do for a few minutes. She watched the other queue for the cheaper seats filing up to box A, and saw that the packets of cigarettes were rapidly diminishing.

Benstead came hurriedly down the stairs from the circle and told her that there were eleven seats at two and nine, and six at two and three. By the time she had issued this number of tickets and was once more temporarily idle, all the packets of cigarettes had been sold. She heard Grace tell a man that they hadn't any.

Another batch of seats in the circle

became vacant, and once more she had a short spasm of being busy. And then, as she issued the last ticket and sat back, she glanced over at box A and saw Grace in the act of selling a twenty-packet of cigarettes to a woman in a fur coat. Eileen felt her heart quicken. The same thing had happened on her first night as second cashier. After Grace had run out of the supply of cigarettes given her by Mr. Benstead, Eileen had seen her produce two further packets from somewhere and sell them. And now she had done the same thing again. Of course, there might not be anything in it; Grace might have merely kept back a few packets for special people whom she knew. On the other hand, there might be quite a lot in it.

Eileen knew now, since her visit to Jonathan Muir's house, what was behind this horrid business that had caused the death of her sister. Was it possible that these mysterious packets of cigarettes, which Grace Singer conjured up from apparently nowhere, did not contain cigarettes at all, but something infinitely more dangerous? It would mean, of course, that Grace was connected with the drug syndicate; but there was nothing impossible in that.

She watched as well as she could in the intervals of issuing tickets, and she saw Grace slip another packet of cigarettes to a well-dressed man who looked ill. She also saw something else. In exchange for the packet of cigarettes, the man had given Grace an envelope. It was done so quickly that unless Eileen had been specially looking for something of the sort, she would never have seen it at all. So she *was* right. Grace Singer was responsible for the distribution of the drugs. She had been doing this for a very long time, and Paula had found her out, threatening to talk unless she was well paid to keep her mouth shut. And because of that, Paula had died . . .

Eileen was so excited about her discovery that it was all she could do to concentrate on her job, but the last of the queue went in eventually and she heaved a sigh of relief.

'All right, Miss Rivers,' said Benstead, 'take your numbers and close box B.

We're issuing all tickets from box A, Foxlow.'

'Right you 'har, sir,' said Mr. Foxlow. 'I don't expect there'll be many more.'

'No,' agreed Benstead, looking at his watch. 'The main feature has been on the screen for fifteen minutes.'

He hurried away to his office, and Eileen, after jotting down the finishing numbers on the automatic ticket machine, collected her money and float and joined Grace in box A.

'Well, dear, that's another day over,' remarked Miss Singer.

'Yes,' said Eileen. 'By the way, have you got any cigarettes? I haven't one left.'

'I'm awfully sorry,' said Grace, 'but I've sold 'em all. We're only allowed ten twenty-packets each night and they went very quickly this evening. You can get some at the cafe down the road.'

She was quite unconcerned. If Eileen had hoped to get any reaction out of her from the mention of cigarettes, she was disappointed.

Rapidly, Grace checked the money and the return book. 'Right,' she said when she had finished, 'you can get off, dear, if you like. I'll take this to Benstead.' She dumped the bags of copper and silver and the wads of notes on the top of the open return book and picked the whole lot up.

'You're sure I can't help you?' asked Eileen, opening the door of the paybox.

'No, you get along. I'm not in a hurry tonight. I think I shall pop in and see the end of the film.'

'I'll just get my hat and coat from the staffroom, then. Good night. See you tomorrow.'

'Good night, dear,' said Grace, and she hurried off to Benstead's office.

Eileen went slowly up the steps to the circle vestibule. She was convinced that for reasons of her own, Miss Singer wanted to get rid of her. Was she meeting someone whom she didn't want Eileen to see? It might be that, or it might be something else. Whatever it was, Eileen was determined that she wasn't going to be got rid of so easily.

She got her coat and hat from the staffroom, but instead of going back the way she had come, she went a few yards up the corridor to where there was a small alcove containing a window. The embrasure was shallow but sufficient to conceal her presence from anybody going into the staffroom.

She waited. After a little while she heard footsteps approaching, the click-clack of high-heeled shoes on the stone floor, and Grace Singer appeared. She went into the women's staffroom, but in a few seconds she came out again — still without her hat and coat, and stood just outside the door hesitantly. It looked, thought Eileen, as though she were waiting for somebody.

The sound of swift footsteps reached her ears, and a man came hurriedly into the corridor. The light was dim but it was sufficient. The man was Harry Stanton!

'All right, give it to me.' Eileen could scarcely catch the words, he spoke in such a low tone, and she saw Grace slip something white into his hand. 'Nothing more till Saturday.'

'I'm scared,' whispered Grace. 'I'm sure that woman was watching me tonight.'

'Which woman?' said Stanton.

'Eileen — Paula's sister. She came here to spy, I know she did.'

'Don't talk here, you little fool.' Stanton's voice was angry. 'I'll meet you in an hour — the usual place.' He turned and walked quickly away, the way he had come, and Grace went back into the staffroom.

Eileen released her pent-up breath in a long, silent sigh. So it was Harry Stanton. He and Grace were working in conjunction. She must follow him. Could she slip past the staffroom door without being seen by Grace? She'd have to risk it.

She tiptoed out of the window recess and along the corridor, silently and apprehensively, scarcely daring to breathe. If Grace came out . . . But she did not, and Eileen reached the safety of the bend in the passage. And then she stopped abruptly.

A few yards ahead of her, Harry Stanton was bending down and inserting a key in the lock of a narrow door built into the wall. Eileen knew that door. Paula had once shown it to her and told her that it led into the space between the sloping floor of the vast circle and the roof of the back stalls called the void. What on earth was Stanton going in there for?

She pressed herself up against the wall, her heart beating wildly. If Grace should come round the corner now, nothing could save her from discovery. They already suspected her of spying, and if they found her here . . . She remembered what had happened to Paula and felt her flesh go cold. Supposing Stanton should look round? He couldn't fail to see her.

He *did* look round at that moment, and at the same instant she heard the hurried click-clack of Grace's heels coming towards her. She was caught between the two of them. Stanton saw her, uttered a startled exclamation, and ran up to her.

'What are you doing here?' he demanded harshly. 'How long have you been there?'

'I — I've just come out of the staffroom . . . ' she began.

'That's a lie,' he broke in. 'You weren't

in the staffroom a second ago. You've been spying!'

'What's the matter?' Grace came round the corner and joined them. 'Oh . . . '

'This woman's been listening. She says she's just come from the staffroom.'

'She wasn't in the staffroom when I first came up,' declared Grace. 'She must've been hiding somewhere.'

'Get a scarf — some rope — anything,' snapped Stanton quickly.

'What are you going to do?' Grace asked.

'You'll see — hurry,' he snapped.

Eileen opened her mouth to scream but he divined her intention, whipped his handkerchief from his breast pocket, and thrust it into her mouth. 'Be quick,' he said over his shoulder to Grace. 'Find something I can tie her up with. Somebody may come along at any minute.'

'Use this.' Grace took off the scarf she had tied round her unruly hair.

'I'll carry her into the void,' said Stanton. 'We can tie her up there. It'll be safer.'

Eileen struggled desperately, but he

half-carried and half-dragged her to the narrow iron door and thrust her inside.

'Shut the door,' he ordered, and Grace slipped inside and obeyed. She pressed a switch and a dim light came on, illuminating the vast semi-circular sweep of the void with the great girders supporting the circle.

Stanton flung Eileen down roughly onto the dusty concrete floor. Then, snatching the scarf from Grace, he bound it round her ankles and knotted it tightly. 'Give me that belt from your coat,' he ordered, and Grace tore it through the loops. Stanton secured Eileen's wrists and arms and stood up, panting.

'There,' he said breathlessly. 'She'll be safe enough until the cinema closes.'

'What are you going to do with her then?' breathed Grace.

'I'm coming back to — finish the job,' whispered Stanton.

28

Mr. Budd Takes Action

Mr. Budd felt restless. He had a sense of frustration that made him irritable. Things were not moving fast enough. Leek had reported nothing of importance from Dorking, and the men who were watching Colonel Hautboy had nothing to report either. Over and over again he went through the facts in his possession, sorting and re-sorting, but getting nowhere. His temper reflected the state of his mind. Little things made him absurdly cross; things that usually wouldn't have bothered him at all. Somehow he had missed an important clue. He had no idea what or where it was, but a vague intuition told him that it had come into his possession and he had passed it by. He had failed, somewhere, to take advantage of an opportunity.

Walking along Whitehall on his way to the Yard, he met Barry Race. 'Hello,' said the gossip writer. 'How are you getting along? Arrested Hautboy yet?'

'You know I 'aven't,' growled Mr. Budd.

'You never will. He's one of the real fly boys. When you get within reach of arresting him, he either won't be there, or you'll be dead.'

'I take a lot o' killin',' said Mr. Budd. 'Somebody tried the other night. Come an' 'ave a drink. Maybe you can tell me somethin'.'

'Not about Hautboy.'

'No.'

They turned into the saloon bar of a nearby public house, and the big man ordered a pint of beer for himself and a double whisky for Race. There was a vacant table in a corner of the bar and they sat down.

'Ever 'eard of a woman called Jacqueline Muir?' asked Mr. Budd abruptly.

'Died from an overdose of heroin,' answered Race promptly. 'Supposed to be suicide. Got mixed up with the smart crowd and found the pace too hot. What about her?'

'She 'ad a friend called Trudi Rhodes,' said Mr. Budd, peering into his tankard. 'D'yer know her?'

'Everybody in the square mile knows her, and nothing at all to her credit. She's always doped to the eyebrows.'

'Dope's at the bottom of this business. The Paula Rivers murder, I mean.'

'That doesn't surprise me. There's been a tremendous increase in it lately. Whoever is running the business must be making a fortune!'

'Hautboy's in it,' said Mr. Budd. 'He isn't the king pippin, but he's in it.' He took a long drink of beer.

'That woman's name isn't Rhodes, really, you know. That's her maiden name.'

'I didn't know she was married. She calls herself Miss.'

'She was divorced two years ago,' said Race. 'The husband was in a band or something. A fellow called Stanton.'

'Say that again,' said Mr. Budd very gently.

'Why? Does it ring a bell?'

'It rings a whole peal.' The stout superintendent swallowed the remainder of his beer at a gulp. 'I'm goin' to get busy.'

He left Barry Race, who was rather astonished at his sudden departure, and went back to the Yard. The assistant commissioner had gone out to lunch and the big man, who was anxious to see him, had to wait in his office until he came back. He filled in the time working out a plan of campaign. The item of information which Barry Race had so casually dropped had acted like a spotlight in a dark night. Harry Stanton, the organist at the Mammoth Cinema, must be this divorced husband of Trudi Rhodes and responsible for the distribution of the drugs. There was no reason why he should not be the unknown head of the entire organization and the murderer of Paula Rivers. He had been one of the people who had been in the circle vestibule during the time the murder must have been committed.

Mr. Budd congratulated himself that he had bought that drink for Barry Race. It had led to more than he had dreamed of suspecting.

As soon as Colonel Blair returned, he went down to his room and made his request. The assistant commissioner looked a little dubious. 'I suppose you know what you're doing?' he said.

Mr. Budd nodded. 'I believe that we shall find a supply o' drugs hidden somewhere in the cinema, an' I want a search warrant.'

'There's going to be a deuce of a row if you don't. You realize that?'

'I don't think there's much risk, sir,' said Mr. Budd. 'I'm pretty sure they're there, and this is the only way to find 'em.'

'When do you propose to conduct the search?'

'Tonight. Just before the place closes, sir. That'll give it the least publicity.'

'All right.' Colonel Blair gave a quick nod with his neat grey head. 'I'll fix the warrant for you. How many men will you want?'

'I shan't want any,' said Mr. Budd. 'I'll arrange with Inspector Longfoot to come with me an' bring Sergeant Ball an' a constable. I think that'll be best, sir.'

'The details are in your hands. I only pray to the Lord you find something!'

'We shall,' said Mr. Budd confidently, and he left the office.

He took his ancient car and drove over to see Longfoot. The inspector listened to what he had to say with interest.

'Are we going to arrest this fellow Stanton?' he asked.

'It depends,' answered Mr. Budd. 'We don't want to do anythin' hasty. We've got no real evidence against 'im, you know.'

'Supposing we find the drugs?'

'There may be nothin' to show he put 'em there. Anybody may have done that. We'll 'ave to go very warily.'

The audience was streaming out when they arrived at the cinema. Mr. Benstead, having changed back to a lounge suit, was standing near the door of his office watching them and talking to a young man whom Mr. Budd recognized as he came up to them. It was Jimmy Redfern, and he looked worried.

'Hello, Superintendent,' said the manager. 'This is rather a late visit, isn't it? I shall be leaving in a minute.'

'I'm afraid you won't, sir,' said Mr. Budd. 'I've got a warrant to search the buildin', an' I shall have to ask you to accompany me.'

'Search the building?' exclaimed Benstead in surprise. 'What on earth for? What do you expect to find?'

'I've reason to believe that this cinema is bein' used as a distributin' centre for dangerous drugs.'

'How did you know that?' broke in Jimmy. 'Have you seen Eileen — Miss Rivers?'

'No.' Mr. Budd looked at him suspiciously.

'Then where can she have got to? She — '

'She left over an hour ago,' put in Benstead. 'I've already told you that.'

'She didn't come out the front way,' said Jimmy. 'I've been waiting for her.'

'She must have left by one of the other exits,' said the manager.

'She wouldn't. She knew I was waiting!'

'Well, she's gone anyhow,' snapped Benstead irritably. 'Look here, what do you mean by drugs?'

'You'll see, sir,' said Mr. Budd. 'Will you fetch your keys, please?'

'Where do you want to go?' demanded Benstead.

'Everywhere,' said Mr. Budd curtly.

The manager led the way into his office. On the wall over the safe was a green baize board on which hung several keys with labels attached. 'Where would you like to start?' he said, with a sweeping gesture toward the board. 'There are all the keys. Help yourself.'

'Thank you, sir,' said Mr. Budd. 'I think . . . ' He stopped as Mr. Foxlow appeared in the doorway.

'They h'are all h'out, sir,' he informed Benstead.

'All right,' said the manager. 'You can go, Foxlow.'

The foreman looked curiously at Mr. Budd, but all he said was: 'Thank you, sir. Don't you want me to put the chains on?'

'No, no,' said Benstead. 'I'll see to it.'

'Good night then, sir,' said Foxlow, and he went out.

Inspector Longfoot and Sergeant Ball came in, and Mr. Budd suggested that they should start their search with the office. They found nothing, but Mr. Budd had not expected to find anything there; it was not the sort of place a supply of drugs would be kept. Next they examined the ticket storeroom behind box A and went up the stairs to the circle. The male staffroom yielded nothing.

'There's only the void and the women's staffroom here,' said Benstead. 'My stock room, where I keep the cigarettes and chocolates, is on the way up to the operating-box.'

'What's the void?' asked Mr. Budd, and the manager explained. 'I'd like to see that,' said the big man with sudden interest. 'I'd like to see that very much indeed.'

Benstead led the way along the corridor and pointed to the narrow iron door. 'There you are,' he said. 'Here's the key.'

Mr. Budd took it, stopped, and inserted it in the lock.

'The switch is just inside,' said Benstead as he opened the door. Mr. Budd felt about and found it. A dim light came on when he pressed it down, and he looked about with interest. The vast place inside the circle was gloomy and full of shadows. An ideal place, he thought, for what he had come to find. And then he heard a sound — a strangled groan that came from somewhere near the floor. Somebody was there, lying near the wall.

He went over quickly and recognized Eileen Rivers. Without wasting any time, he pulled the handkerchief from her mouth, and as she saw who it was the fear faded from her eyes.

'Oh,' she said, faintly. 'Thank God it's you.'

'Eileen!' Jimmy Redfern, outside the open door, had heard her. He came in quickly, brushed Mr. Budd aside, and knelt down. 'Eileen. How did you get here? Are you hurt . . . ?'

'It was Stanton . . . Stanton and Grace.'

'Stanton . . . *Harry* Stanton?' he demanded incredulously.

'Yes . . . and Grace. They caught me watching them, and . . . Stanton's coming back. He may be here any moment.'

Mr. Budd took a knife from his pocket and cut through the scarf and belt that bound her. 'If he does, we'll deal with him, miss,' he said. 'Don't you worry. Can you stand, d'you think?'

'Yes.' She got up with Redfern's help. 'I'm all right, only frightened.'

Mr. Budd called to Sergeant Ball. 'Take her down to the office,' he said. 'I'll have a word with you, miss, after we've finished here.'

'I'll come with you, Eileen,' said Jimmy. 'I was afraid something like this would happen.'

'Were you, now?' remarked Mr. Budd. 'I think I'd like a word with you too, Mr. Redfern . . . Look after them both, Sergeant.'

'This is incredible,' broke in Benstead. 'You can't mean that Stanton, my organist, was responsible for tying this woman up here?'

'I can,' said Mr. Budd grimly, 'an' for quite a lot of other things, too.'

'There's somebody over there,' said Longfoot sharply. 'Right over on the far side.'

A report echoed through the void and they saw a vicious stab of flame. A bullet whined past Mr. Budd's head and smacked into the wall.

'Get through that door — all of you!' snarled the big man. 'There's — '

His words were drowned by the crash of a second shot, which was followed instantly by a third and a fourth. Benstead uttered a yelp of terror and skipped out the doorway.

Mr. Budd dropped flat on his face and wriggled his way towards the exit. He was unarmed, and it would be suicide to try and tackle the unknown with the automatic. A bullet struck the concrete floor near his face and he felt the splinters settle over his head.

'Is there another exit to this place?' he gasped as he reached the doorway.

'No,' answered Benstead from the corridor. 'This is the only way in or out.'

Mr. Budd gathered himself for a final effort, sprang to his feet, and jumped through the doorway. Three shots followed him, and then he slammed the door shut and locked it. 'That's settled him,' he panted. 'If there's no other way, he can't get out.'

'Who was it, Stanton?' said Longfoot.

Before Mr. Budd could reply, there was the sound of a shout and a shot from somewhere below.

29

The Man Who Came Out

'What's happening now?' muttered Benstead, his face white.

'You stay 'ere,' snapped Mr. Budd to Longfoot, 'an' keep an eye on that door. 'E may try and shoot his way out. I'll find out what's goin' on.'

He hurried away. When he reached the circle vestibule, he saw three people struggling desperately at the foot of the staircase and recognized one of them as Stanton. Sergeant Ball and the constable were trying to wrest a pistol from the organist's hand while Eileen and Jimmy looked on. Mr. Budd pounded down the stairs, seized the hand that held the automatic and gave it a twist. Stanton uttered a grunt of pain and the weapon fell on the floor.

'All right,' panted Mr. Budd, picking it

up quickly, 'put the 'cuffs on 'im, one of you.'

They had all their work cut out, for Stanton fought like a demon, but they managed it.

'You're under arrest,' said the big man. 'The charge for the moment is assaultin' Miss Eileen Rivers with intent to do bodily harm, but there'll be others. Anythin' you say may be used in evidence.'

But Stanton said nothing. The fight had gone out of him, and he only glared sullenly at them.

'Look after 'im,' said Mr. Budd. 'I'm goin' back to find out who's in the void. I'm feelin' better now I've got this.' He waved the automatic and hurried back up the stairs. Longfoot looked at him questioningly when he reached the locked door to the void.

'They've got Stanton,' said Mr. Budd breathlessly.

'*Stanton?*' said the inspector. 'Then who's in there?'

'That's what we're goin' ter find out,' grunted Mr. Budd. 'It's not goin' ter be so one-sided this time.'

'You can't go in there,' said Longfoot. 'You'd make too good a target!'

'We're goin' ter use a bit o' strategy,' remarked the big man softly. 'Now you just listen ter me.'

The man crouching behind the door inside the void listened with straining ears. There was still somebody outside. He could hear them moving about, and the dull murmur of voices. Dare he make a dash for it? He might be able to shoot his way through, but there were many of them, and he might fail to make a getaway. He had been a fool to take the risk of coming here in the first place, but the chance to get Budd had been too good to miss. He cursed the bad luck that had let the fat man get away. With Budd out of the picture he would have been safe — completely safe. Budd was the only danger. There was nothing whatever to connect him with the drugs racket, and he'd made enough money out of it not to bother that it was finished.

He stiffened suddenly. The muffled sound of shouting reached his ears. The voice was Budd's, and it sounded far away.

'Longfoot, Longfoot, come 'ere — quickly.'

The inspector answered from immediately outside the door: 'What about watching this door?'

'Never mind,' called Mr. Budd's voice impatiently. ''E can't get far. Come 'ere quickly.'

The listening man heard running footsteps rapidly retreating. It was now or never. If he could make his way to the roof, he could get down by the fire escape. He pulled the handkerchief back up over his face and opened the door. As he stepped through into the passage, something struck him across the hand in which he held the pistol. As he dropped it with a cry of pain, two men closed on him from either side of the doorway.

'Got you!' cried Inspector Longfoot triumphantly.

The prisoner struggled violently, but his strength was no match for the combined efforts of Inspector Longfoot and Sergeant Ball. They twisted his arms expertly behind his back and soon had him helpless.

Mr. Budd came panting along the corridor. 'So it worked, did it?' he remarked. 'Now let's 'ave a look at yer.'

He pulled the concealing handkerchief from the man's face, and Churchman glared at him with murder in his eyes.

★   ★   ★

Mr. Budd was a very busy man for the rest of that night. Harry Stanton and Churchman were taken to the police station with a strong guard headed by Sergeant Ball, and Grace Singer was arrested in the Greek restaurant up the road where she was awaiting the return of Stanton. In her handbag they found over a hundred pounds in one-pound notes, and concealed in a twenty-packet of Player's cigarettes a small marcasite box full of cocaine. A search of the void resulted in the discovery of a vast quantity of drugs, all separately packed in the little marcasite boxes, and hidden inside cigarette packets.

'There's thousands o' quid's worth of stuff 'ere,' said Mr. Budd when he had examined the stock. 'This was their principal storehouse, I should think.'

The horrified Mr. Benstead, who had accompanied them on their inspection, shook his head in rather a dazed manner.

'I never suspected anything of the kind,' he said. 'We seldom go into the void, except for a perfunctory inspection. I don't know what my head office will have to say.'

Mr. Budd thought that whatever it was, it was scarcely likely to be complimentary to Mr. Benstead, but he didn't say so. The little manager looked worried enough already.

'Let's go down to the station an' see if those birds'll sing,' he said.

'Couldn't I take Miss Rivers home?' said Jimmy. 'She's had a pretty bad time.'

'Yes,' agreed Mr. Budd. 'But I shall want to see yer both first thin' in the mornin'. You'd better be at the station at nine-thirty.'

They promised to be there, and Mr. Budd left them outside the cinema and made his way to the police station with Longfoot.

Two of the 'birds' sang very loudly. Grace Singer and Harry Stanton made long statements that were signed and witnessed, but Churchman refused to say anything.

'I insist upon my lawyer being sent for,' he said.

'We'll send for 'im,' said Mr. Budd. 'But you won't get away with it, Churchman. I want you for murder an' attempted murder, an' no lawyer is goin' to get you out of it.'

'Whose murder?' demanded Churchman.

'Paula Rivers's,' snapped Mr. Budd laconically, and he went to the telephone to put through a long call to Scotland Yard.

As a direct result of this, a big police car drew up shortly afterwards outside The Talking Parrot, and several men from headquarters forced their way into Colonel Hautboy's flat and took that protesting gentleman away with them to Cannon Row, where he was charged and spent the remainder of the night uncomfortably in a cell.

'That's that,' yawned Mr. Budd wearily when the message came through that Hautboy had been arrested. 'That's pretty near everythin'. All we want is the Whisperin' Woman.'

'How does she come into it?' said Longfoot.

Mr. Budd shook his head. 'I don't know. Stanton 'asn't said anythin' about 'er in his statement, nor 'as Singer.'

'Perhaps Churchman knows?'

'Maybe 'e does, but he isn't talking,' grunted Mr. Budd. 'What about some coffee, eh? I could do with somethin'.'

'Come down to the canteen,' said the inspector. 'I'm going to have a spot of food.'

They did so, and dawn was breaking when they came back to the inspector's office. Mr. Budd had hardly settled himself in the only comfortable chair, with a prodigious yawn, when a constable put his head round the door.

'Excuse me, sir,' he said, 'but there's a man 'ere wants to see you.'

'Me?' said Mr. Budd.

'Yes, sir. Sup'n'tendent Budd 'e asked for, sir.'

'Shoot 'im in,' grunted the big man briefly.

There was a slight pause, and then the constable returned with a small wizened man with a wrinkled face that was curiously reminiscent of Punch. He regarded Mr. Budd with a pair of small beady eyes that twinkled humorously.

'Good morning, sir,' he greeted the superintendent. 'I hear you've beaten me to it.'

'Beaten you to what?' demanded Mr. Budd.

'This drug business. You've got Stanton, Singer, Hautboy and the king pippin — Churchman. Very good going, sir, if I may say so. I congratulate you.'

'Look 'ere, what's this all about?' growled Mr. Budd. 'Who are you?'

'The name is Stubbins,' replied the little man with a beaming smile that showed almost toothless jaws. 'Nicholas Stubbins — private investigator. At your service, sir.'

30

The Whispering Woman

Mr. Stubbins laid a neat card on the desk in front of the surprised Mr. Budd. 'What's all this got to do with me?' inquired the big man sleepily.

'I rather think you've been looking for me,' said Mr. Stubbins. 'In fact, if I may say so, most of the police force have been looking for me. When Mr. Redfern telephoned a couple of hours ago and told me what had happened, I concluded it was time I put in an appearance.'

'You mean . . . ?' Mr. Budd sat up as a light flickered in his tired brain.

'I am the 'old woman' in the case,' said Mr. Stubbins. 'One of my most successful disguises, if I may say so!'

Mr. Budd surveyed him severely. 'You'd better do a bit of explainin',' he grunted. 'If you're the person the whole

perlice force 'as been lookin' for, why
didn't yer come forward before?'

'It wouldn't have helped you.'

'That was for us to decide. I'm not at
all sure that I oughtn't to charge yer with
obstructin' the perlice in the execution of
their duty. 'Owever, let's 'ear what you've
got to say.'

Mr. Nicholas Stubbins looked round,
saw an empty chair, pulled it towards him
and sat down. 'That's what I'm here for,'
he said. 'Well, I came into this business
about a year ago. I was engaged by Mr.
Muir to inquire into the death of his
daughter.'

'Why didn't 'e go to the police?' asked
Mr. Budd.

'He didn't have much faith in the
police,' said Mr. Stubbins. 'Mind you,' he
added hastily, 'I don't agree with him. I
think the police are wonderful.'

'You sound like an American film star,'
said Mr. Budd. 'Never mind the bou-
quets. Get on with it.'

'It was Mr. Muir's opinion,' continued
Mr. Stubbins, 'that the death of his
daughter was neither an accident nor

suicide. He was convinced that she'd been murdered.'

'Why didn't 'e say so at the inquest?'

'Well, of course, that would have been the right thing to do, but he didn't want to let the people responsible think he was suspicious. He was afraid it 'ud put them on their guard. There was really no evidence, you see.'

'So 'e engaged you to try an' find some,' grunted Mr. Budd, nodding. 'Did you?'

'Well, no,' admitted Mr. Stubbins, 'but I did get onto this drug syndicate, or whatever you like to call it. I think, if I may say so, that I rather got ahead of the police. It was quite a piece of luck, really. You see, I knew about Trudi Rhodes, and that it was through her that Jacqueline Muir acquired her drug habit. I found out about her divorce, and that led me to Stanton and the Mammoth Cinema. It also led me to The Talking Parrot, because I was tailing him on the several occasions when he took Paula Rivers there.'

'It was Stanton who took the gal there,

was it?' remarked Mr. Budd.

Stubbins nodded. 'Yes. It was when they were saying good night — the night before she was killed — that I overheard her say to Stanton: 'It'll cost you five thousand pounds if you want me to keep my mouth shut.' I guessed she'd found out something and was putting the black on him. I tried to warn her by sending that note by her sister, but it was too late.'

'Did you rope in Eileen, Redfern and Nicholls to 'elp you?' inquired Mr. Budd.

Again Stubbins nodded. 'They saw me going down to Muir's house in a car and followed. I was in the 'old woman' disguise. Nicholls was nosing round the house and was caught by Muir's chauffeur.' He explained what had happened that night. 'We told them the whole story and they agreed to help. It was I who suggested that Eileen should get a job at the cinema and try and find out what she could. I didn't tell her anything about Stanton.'

'Or Churchman,' murmured Mr. Budd. 'Or perhaps you didn't know anything about Churchman?'

'Yes, I did,' replied Mr. Stubbins complacently. 'I didn't miss much, if I may say so. I knew that Foxlow and Churchman were one and the same. I'd followed him one night to that West End flat of his. You see, I wanted to know all I could about all the people who worked at the Mammoth. I trailed most of the men at one time or another, but Stanton and Foxlow were the only ones who were at all suspicious. I put a man on to break into Foxlow's flat and try and force something out of him.'

'That was the feller who bumped into me, I suppose?' said Mr. Budd.

'Was it you?' Mr. Stubbins smiled, which Mr. Budd thought was a ghastly sight. 'He told me he bumped into *somebody* in his hurry to get away. You see, I knew quite a lot, but I hadn't got any real evidence against these people. If — '

'*I* may say so,' interrupted Mr. Budd, 'you seem to have been a very busy little fellow. What you ought to 'ave done was ter come to us an' told us all you knew. Well, you'd better write out a statement, an' of course we'll need you as a witness.'

'I shall be pleased to do anything I can,' said Mr Stubbins. 'That's why I came at once when I heard what had happened.' He chuckled, a cackling little sound that was most disagreeable. 'I've given a great many people a lot to think about.'

'You've given a great many people a lot o' trouble,' said Mr. Budd severely. 'The problem with you was that your investigation was too private.'

The telephone rang and he picked up the receiver. Leek's voice came faintly over the wire. 'I've been tryin' to get yer everywhere,' complained the sergeant plaintively. 'Somethin's happened.'

'You're tellin' me,' said Mr. Budd.

'A feller left Muir's house about three hours ago in a car,' said Leek. 'A queer-lookin' feller.'

'I know,' interrupted Mr. Budd impatiently. 'He's sittin' in front o' me at the moment. As usual, yer a bit late. You can pack up an' come back. The case is over bar the shoutin'.'

* * *

Three days later, Mr. Budd made a final report to the assistant commissioner. 'Well, sir,' he said wearily, 'I've got all the loose ends tied up now. Churchman was the 'ead of the bunch, but he worked it so cleverly that nobody knew 'im — not even Stanton an' Singer. All 'is orders was given over the telephone, an' 'e got 'em together in the same way, an' 'e 'ad some kind of an 'old on all of 'em — somethin' they'd done which 'ud get 'em in bad trouble if they was given away. As Foxlow 'e was able to keep a personal eye on the cinema end, which was the most important because it was the distributin' end and also their main store. Stanton was in charge o' this, workin' with Grace Singer. The drugs was put up in small marcasite boxes an' concealed inside packets of cigarettes. There was a password which was changed for every distribution. When a customer asked for a ticket, 'e or she mentioned this password and was given what looked like a packet of cigarettes an' paid over the agreed price, which varied accordin' to the drug.'

'Ingenious,' murmured Colonel Blair.

'The whole thing was ingenious,' said Mr. Budd. 'Paula Rivers got onto it, though, an' threatened to give the game away unless they paid up. She wanted five thousand pounds to keep 'er mouth shut, but they knew she wouldn't stop at that. Stanton reported the matter to his unknown chief — Churchman — an' that settled Paula's goose. Churchman shot 'er with an air-pistol from the circle vestibule.'

'How do you know it was Churchman?' asked the assistant commissioner.

'When I called on Churchman the night that feller from Stubbins knocked me flyin', Churchman 'ad to account fer 'is masqueradin' as 'Foxlow' at the Mammoth Cinema. 'E knew there was no use pretendin' I'd made a mistake, so 'e said 'e'd bin loaned by MI5 ter the Foreign Office ter investigate the drug traffic. 'E bolstered up 'is story by producin' the warrant issued to all Intelligence Officers. It was the real thin', an' I admit I was completely taken in. I accepted 'is story, an' when he asked me to keep it confidential, I agreed.'

'Surely he ran a considerable risk. If you had checked up on him, you would have found his story to be false.'

'Yes, sir,' murmured Mr. Budd. 'An', of course, that's what I should 'ave done. But the warrant card was the genuine article, an' they ain't easy to come by.'

'How did he come by it?'

'It belonged to 'is brother. 'E really was in MI5, an' he was killed in a blitz. 'E'd left 'is warrant card be'ind when he changed his clothes that night. He also left somethin' else — a souvenir 'e'd brought back from Germany — a Deloraine air-pistol.'

'The weapon that killed Paula Rivers?' said the assistant commissioner.

'Yes, sir,' said Mr. Budd. 'An' I think it's goin' ter hang 'im.'

★ ★ ★

'I like this place better than The Talking Parrot,' said Eileen.

'The Talking Parrot's closed,' said George Nicholls.

'So far as I'm concerned it can remain

so,' remarked Jimmy Redfern. 'I hated the place and that grinning chap, Hautboy.'

'I'll bet he isn't grinning now,' said Nicholls. He looked at Eileen. 'Shall we dance?'

'This is *my* dance,' put in Jimmy promptly. 'Isn't it, Eileen?'

'If you like.' She smiled and got up.

Nicholls shrugged his shoulders and watched them as they mingled with the dancers on the floor.

'You didn't mind?' said Jimmy as he deftly steered his partner through the throng. 'My butting in on Nicholls like that, I mean?'

'He dances very well,' she said.

'He does most things very well,' grunted Jimmy. 'Would you like me to take you back . . . ?'

'Don't be silly.'

'Eileen,' he said after a long pause, 'Nicholls wanted to dance with you because he wanted to . . . to . . . '

'Wanted to what?' she asked, though she knew very well.

'To ask you to marry him.' Jimmy was red and flustered. 'If he . . . if he does ask you, what will you say?'

'No,' she answered promptly.

He gave a sigh of relief, and she felt his arm tighten about her.

'Supposing . . . ' He gulped and then went on very quickly: 'Supposing *I* asked you . . . ?'

'I should say yes,' she said calmly.

'Oh, that's wonderful!' he exclaimed, and stopped.

'Well, why don't you?' she inquired.

'Why don't I what?'

'Ask me.' She smiled.

GRIM DEATH
MURDER IN MANUSCRIPT
THE GLASS ARROW
THE THIRD KEY
THE ROYAL FLUSH MURDERS
THE SQUEALER
MR. WHIPPLE EXPLAINS
THE SEVEN CLUES
THE CHAINED MAN
THE HOUSE OF THE GOAT
THE FOOTBALL POOL MURDERS
THE HAND OF FEAR
SORCERER'S HOUSE
THE HANGMAN
THE CON MAN
MISTER BIG
THE JOCKEY
THE SILVER HORSESHOE
THE TUDOR GARDEN MYSTERY
THE SHOW MUST GO ON
SINISTER HOUSE
THE WITCHES' MOON
ALIAS THE GHOST
THE LADY OF DOOM
THE BLACK HUNCHBACK

PHANTOM HOLLOW
WHITE WIG
THE GHOST SQUAD
THE NEXT TO DIE

with Chris Verner:
THE BIG FELLOW

We do hope that you have enjoyed reading this large print book.

Did you know that all of our titles are available for purchase?

We publish a wide range of high quality large print books including:
Romances, Mysteries, Classics
General Fiction
Non Fiction and Westerns

Special interest titles available in large print are:
The Little Oxford Dictionary
Music Book, Song Book
Hymn Book, Service Book

Also available from us courtesy of Oxford University Press:
Young Readers' Dictionary
(large print edition)
Young Readers' Thesaurus
(large print edition)

For further information or a free brochure, please contact us at:
Ulverscroft Large Print Books Ltd.,
The Green, Bradgate Road, Anstey,
Leicester, LE7 7FU, England.
Tel: (00 44) **0116 236 4325**
Fax: (00 44) **0116 234 0205**